TOPAZ ISLAND

Phillida Bethel's first holiday job is mother's help to beautiful Suzanne Kingley on the exotic Topaz Island. But she could never have guessed that danger, romance, adventure and excitement are to come her way — in full measure. And her inexperience leaves her with no yardstick by which to assess the fascinating American boy, Jeff Aymon. It is the English student, Greg Somerville, who seems the only safe haven in a world of beauty which suddenly turns sinister . . .

PATRICIA ROBINS

TOPAZ ISLAND

Complete and Unabridged

LINFORD
Leicester

First published in Great Britain in 1965

First Linford Edition
published 2009

British Library CIP Data

Robins, Patricia, *1921* –
    Topaz Island - - (Linford romance library)
    1. Romantic suspense novels.
    2. Large type books.
    I. Title II. Series
    823.9'14–dc22

    ISBN 978–1–84782–833–0

Published by
F. A. Thorpe (Publishing)
Anstey, Leicestershire

Set by Words & Graphics Ltd.
Anstey, Leicestershire
Printed and bound in Great Britain by
T. J. International Ltd., Padstow, Cornwall

This book is printed on acid-free paper

1

It was only now, when all the exams and interviews were over and she finally knew for certain that she had a place at Bristol University in the autumn, that Phillida thought about the holiday job she must get if she were to make ends meet.

'Surely this dress will do!' Granny Bethel said, holding up the hideous item of school uniform which Phillida hoped never to have to wear again.

'Oh, Granny, no. I can't wear that!' Phil tried to curb her impatience. Perhaps a mother might have understood about fashion but Granny, bless her heart, simply hadn't a clue.

'I can't see why not, dear. It looks perfectly good to me.' Granny looked at her seventeen-year-old granddaughter with her customary twin feelings of anxiety and bewilderment.

Phillida was two whole generations away — and long generations, for her father had been born when Granny Bethel was thirty, and he had been thirty when Phillida was born.

Sixty years was too big a gap to be breached for full understanding but nevertheless, each was deeply devoted to the other.

Both Phillida's parents had died in an aeroplane accident in America. She had been only two years old at the time and Granny Bethel had never suspected that when she offered to look after the little girl for two weeks that it was to mean for the rest of her lifetime. Fortunately for them both, Phillida was endowed not only with good looks but with an exceptionally high I.Q. Neither of her parents had carried life insurance and there was so little saved at the time of their death that Phillida's only hope of a good education was to earn it through the state schooling system. She passed both her O levels and A levels a year younger than the average. Now, after years of intensely hard work, she had gained her university entrance and was to realise her ambition to study languages in which she hoped to obtain a degree.

It had not been easy for the old woman to bring up this brilliant child. Her own education had been very brief and she had long since forgotten what she had learned at school. She was powerless to help the little girl with difficult algebra problems or Latin homework and could only stand aside, bewildered and anxious, as the child was forced to rely on her own ability.

There had been little or no time for any kind of social life. Phil's studies had occupied most of her evenings and weekends. In the holidays, she would go out with her girlfriends and very occasionally to a party, but there had been no steady boyfriend. For this Granny Bethel was thankful, for she was not at all sure she would have known how to guide Phil. As far as she knew, Phil, at seventeen, was completely innocent and, moreover, disinterested in most of the modern teenage activities.

In fact, this was not entirely true. Phil had longed for a stereo system, a tape deck, the latest records and friends in to dance to them, but she knew only too well the enormous financial sacrifices Granny Bethel was continually making, in order to keep her in school uniform and books and pocket money. She simply could not and would not ask for luxuries.

But now she knew that at least a few fashionable clothes and accessories were essential — no longer to be thought of as a luxury, and that since she couldn't ask Granny Bethel for money, she must get a job for the next six months to enable her to buy what she needed.

Gently she tried to make Granny Bethel understand that work was no hardship for her; that she was quite old enough now to look after herself away from home; that she must earn some money to buy what she needed for the more sophisticated surroundings of university life.

'That dress is, and only could be, school uniform!' she explained. 'Anyway, Granny, it's far too tight for me now.'

Her grandmother sighed.

'I do wish I could help somehow, Phillida!' (She never shortened Phil's name.) 'Somehow I don't like the idea of you working. You need a rest, dear. You've been working so hard for so long — and you look tired.'

Phil gave her reflection in the mirror a swift glance and hurriedly looked away again. Her hair was badly in need of a good cut. Her face did look drawn — some make-up would help. She would have liked to have bought some new cosmetics as well as a new wardrobe of clothes and shoes. She knew she had long, pretty legs, but couldn't do them justice in last year's school skirts.

'I shall get the kind of job where I

don't have to use my brains, Granny!' she said, her slanting green eyes sparkling with sudden amusement. The corners of her rather too-big mouth also turned upwards, giving her an impish look. 'I'll be a mother's help — you know I'm domestically qualified. And minding children will be a piece of cake for me after being a prefect for a year.'

It took Granny a week or two to get used to the idea and by that time Phil had lined up a job. She came back from the interview with her future employer, filled with excitement and enthusiasm.

'Oh, Granny, I do wish you could have come with me. Mrs. Kingley is perfectly sweet — and miles younger than I'd expected. I don't think she can be more than about thirty-five at the most. And her clothes — Granny, they were absolutely gorgeous. She was wearing a lovely leather suit and she has beautiful blonde hair. I think she must have been a model or something. You can tell from the way she walks.'

Granny Bethel broke in:

'But what will you have to do, Phillida?'

'Practically nothing!' Phil said, her green eyes shining. 'And I'm being paid fifty pounds a week for the privilege!' She caught the old woman round the waist and hugged her. 'I've really been lucky, Gran. She nearly engaged a foreign girl yesterday and then decided to hold back the letter of acceptance until she'd seen me.'

Phil dropped exhausted into the shabby old sofa. She could not fully believe in her good luck. Mrs. Kingley had been so sweet.

'It'll be such fun for us both!' she had said — not like an employer at all. 'May I call you Phil? And you must call me Suzanne. I do wish the children were here for you to meet but they are both at a birthday party. Jenny is eight and Rupert is one. I think you'll find them easy to manage. I had a Scots nanny since Jenny was born but she left to get married. I don't want to get another nanny yet because I'm not certain where my husband is going to be sent. He's in the Foreign Office and he's due for a term abroad but we just don't know where. At the moment he's in America. So you see, you coming for six months fits in perfectly with our plans and I do hope you will decide to take the job.'

Phil had not hesitated. The London house where Mrs. Kingley lived was beautiful. The room Phil was to have had seemed, by comparison with her own shabby room in Granny's council flat in Camden, fit for a princess. The children's nursery quarters consisted of day and night rooms and their own bathroom, all decorated in yellow and white.

Mrs. Kingley had smiled at her gasps of admiration.

'You want to see our home on Topaz Island — it's far more attractive than this!' she said.

'Topaz Island?'

'Yes! It's just off the coast of the

South of France. We go there in March and stay till it gets too hot in July or August. You won't mind going abroad?'

'Granny, I'll be going abroad — to France!' Phil cried. 'I shall be able to improve my accent and learn a whole lot. It's just all too good to be true!'

Granny smiled, pleased that Phillida was so happy and excited and relieved to know that she would be going to live with such nice people.

'I told Mrs. Kingley you couldn't get about much because of your rheumatism and she said she'd come and pay you a visit, Granny, just so that you'll know who I shall be going to live with. Isn't that nice of her? And, Granny, look!'

In her excitement, Phil had forgotten one of the most important happenings of the day. She reached into her handbag and pulled out a slip of paper.

'It's a cheque — for a hundred pounds. One hundred pounds, Gran. Two weeks' salary in advance, Mrs. Kingley said, in case I needed to buy clothes. Wasn't that thoughtful of her? Oh, I'm so happy I could burst!'

'She does know you are inexperienced?' Granny Bethel asked anxiously. 'You seem very young to be getting so much money.'

'Yes, I know, but she does know!' Phil said confusedly. 'And she doesn't want references; she says my school reports are quite enough. And, Granny, she's glad I'm not a trained nanny — she said her previous one had been fearfully bossy and had often kept her away from the children and she'd hated it, so it's all all right. As for the money — I think they must have so much, fifty pounds a week is nothing to them. You should see the house, Granny — it's amazing. It looks as if it's all been furnished and decorated regardless of cost. And they must be rich, anyway, to have their own villa in France. Doesn't it sound perfect, Gran? Topaz Island?'

What Phil did not yet know was that the Kingleys owned not just the villa but the whole five square miles of Topaz

Island. But this was only one thing among many she did not know . . . for instance, that Mr. Kingley was twenty years older than his wife; he had been married before to a wealthy American woman who had died leaving him a fortune and the guardianship of a stepson by her own previous marriage; that Jeff Aymon was at this very moment packing his belongings at his American college from which he had finally been sent down in disgrace.

2

The train journey to New York might have been a lot more tedious for Jeff if he had not met up with a very pretty actress who had been delighted to permit the attractive young college boy to entertain her. And Jeff Aymon could be very entertaining when he chose.

He was what an Englishman would call typically American to look at. He was tall and beautifully built with square shoulders and narrow hips. Even the close crew-cut could not diminish entirely the blue-black shine of his dark hair. Beneath a broad wide forehead his eyes shone surprisingly blue. It was an open honest attractive face; a face one instinctively trusted and liked. It was Jeff's biggest asset.

In his pocket was a letter for his stepfather from the principal of his college. He knew very well what was in it; knew too, that on no account could he permit his stepfather to read it. Deliberately, he tore it into tiny squares and let them fall out of the window.

'Say, honey, what's that you're doing?'

Jeff grinned at his travelling companion.

'Getting rid of my past!' he said.

'Oh, a love-letter. What happened, honey? Did she let you down?'

'Not quite. She found me out! Now, how about another drink to celebrate?'

Two hours later Jeff was drinking yet another Scotch — this time in the company of his stepfather. So far, Charles Kingley had not been very friendly. In fact, he'd been definitely distant, Jeff thought. It was time he altered that. He said:

'I know this must be a pretty nasty shock for you, but frankly, when you hear what really happened, I don't think you'll blame me!'

Charles Kingley looked at his stepson with misgivings. The boy had been six when his mother had died and, like a lot of American children, hopelessly spoilt by English standards. Charles had never actually liked the boy — never managed to get close to him but he'd put this down to the fact that he himself was rather shy, introverted and typically English, and that he had little in common with this stepson who, he supposed, took after his French father rather than his American mother. Already in his late forties when Jeff was born, the Frenchman had died a year after his son's birth, leaving his far younger widow the opportunity to marry again. Charles had taken on the responsibility for the boy when he married his mother.

Because Jeff had wanted it so passionately, Charles had arranged for him to stay at school in America when his own spell of duty in Washington was up and he had to return to England. There had been Aunt Georgie on his mother's side who was prepared to act as his guardian and Jeff would be sent to England for the longest vacation. When the time came, however, Jeff had not wanted to leave. Aunt Georgie had written a long rambling letter about summer camp and Jeff's friends and because he, Charles, was already in love with Suzanne by then and wishing to spend as much of his spare time as possible with her, he allowed the boy to stay in the States.

The cable from the aunt asking him to come to America as soon as he could had been a nasty shock. He had been in regular correspondence with her and as far as he knew, Jeff had been in no trouble over the years since he had last seen him. Now, like a bombshell, he learned that the boy was being expelled from his college.

He got leave from the office and flew to America. From New York he telephoned Aunt Georgie. She refused to give details on the telephone and told him Jeff would be arriving next day and would come to his hotel and explain everything.

And here the boy was — no, not a boy any longer, a young man, self-assured, even a little tough at first summing up — and apparently not one whit ashamed of himself for being chucked out of college.

'It was like this, sir!'

Charles listened to the American accent, trying to accustom his ears to the sudden change from home. 'This buddy of mine and I were taking two girls for a spin. We'd had a few drinks and I suppose Hank must have had more than I thought. Anyway, he was jumping mad to drive my car when it came time to go home. First off, I refused, then I said okay because this kid has come through school the hard way — no dough, you understand? Works his way. Well, next thing we hit a tree and there's this girl, my date as a matter of fact, pretty badly hurt. Hank is frantic. 'If they find out it's me who was driving, there'll be all hell let loose,' he said. 'I haven't a licence and I've no insurance.''

16

Jeff leaned back in his chair, regarding his stepfather closely.

'Well, what would you have done, sir? He was my buddy and it was partly my fault for letting him drive. So we swapped seats and sat there till the first car passed by.'

'And the girl?'

'Well, that's the awful part, sir. She wasn't killed but she was quite badly injured. There was a court case and I took the blame and my aunt thought it best to notify you.'

Charles let out his breath. Unknown to himself, he had been sitting tensely, holding himself taut until he realised that far from being in disgrace, Jeff had done rather a fine thing. Of course, it was crazy for the boy to take the blame for anything so serious. If this girl had died, there could have been an action for manslaughter. Still, mercifully it hadn't come to that.

'Frankly, sir,' Jeff said, 'I'm not too sorry. I've just about had college anyway and I'd rather like to get a job of some sort — to give me something worthwhile to do. I thought maybe I might take you up on that ten-year-old offer to visit England, educate myself that way. What do you think, sir?'

'Of course!' Charles said at once. 'You realise, I suppose, that you don't have to get a job? Your mother left enough money for me to give you a fairly generous allowance.'

The boy nodded.

'Yeah. I know the terms of my mother's will — Aunt Georgie showed me her copy. You got the capital and I get part of the interest till you die, or something. All the same, I think I should work, don't you, sir? It's better for a man to have a job of some kind.'

Charles looked at the boy with growing interest. He might look like his French father but he had some of his American mother's sound common sense.

'I think you've earned a holiday first,' he said. 'That must have been a pretty unpleasant affair for you to have to go through. I wish I'd known earlier — I'd have come out.'

'My aunt wanted to contact you but I was afraid you might want Hank to own up. He'd had a pretty rough time and he owes it to his family to get through college. Besides, I was partly to blame — letting him drive, and paying for all the drinks — I ought to have known better.'

'Well, if nothing else, you'll have learned your lesson,' Charles said. 'Now, let's have some dinner, Jeff, and then we'll see about reservations for the first plane home. I'm anxious for you to meet my wife — Suzanne. You'll like her, I know. And my two children. In a few weeks' time, we all go off to the South of France to our island there. But of course, you know about that, I expect. It belonged to your mother.'

'Yes, I know all about Topaz Island!' Jeff's voice had become suddenly quiet, lazy, almost disinterested. His college professor could have told Charles that this was a deliberate mask, put on whenever Jeff's interest was most widely awake. 'Yes, sir. I'd like very much to visit there.'

Charles suddenly shivered.

'I can't get used to your air-conditioning in the States!' he said smilingly. 'Always makes me feel cold.'

'But it'll be warm on Topaz Island!' Jeff said softly. 'A little too warm, perhaps.'

Charles answered this remark literally.

'Later in the summer, yes. But the next few months are quite perfect. Suzanne, my wife, loves going there; the children, too. I only wish I could spend more time with them. I'm lucky indeed to get a whole month there.'

'I'll tell Aunt Georgie!' Jeff said, rising suddenly to his feet with a quick unexpected action that was peculiar to him. One moment he would be quiet, relaxed, seeming almost asleep — and the next quick, darting, light on his feet. 'Like a lizard' one of his friends had once described him.

'I thought maybe I should go and see her,' Charles began, but Jeff broke in:

'Do we have to, sir? You see, I didn't dare tell her the truth about that accident for fear she would get poor old Hank involved, so she naturally blames me and feels pretty sore about it all. I — I think it would only distress her to go over it all again; and to see me. I think she'd be much happier just to know you were going to be looking after me for a while.'

Charles hesitated. He had no particular desire to see this woman whom he scarcely knew except by letter. Perhaps Jeff was right and the best thing was to get off back to England. In any case, he hated being parted from Suzanne and the children longer than necessary, especially now that she was alone in the house except for the Italian cook. He'd be glad when she found a replacement for Nanny . . .

He turned his thoughts back to the boy and nodded.

'Go ahead, then, Jeff, and telephone

your aunt. While you're gone, I'll order dinner.'

★ ★ ★

Jeff leaned against the wall of the hotel phone booth and stared at the girl who was trying to connect him to Aunt Georgie. The girl was small, dark and pretty and was enjoying the flirtation as much as he was. If only his stepfather wasn't here, he'd . . .

'Your call is through, sir!'

'Aunt Georgie?'

'Oh, Jeff! Where are you? I've been so worried. Why didn't you call me sooner? I waited in all yesterday after they told me at the college you'd gone and I've not had a wink of sleep . . .'

'Cut it out, Aunt Georgie. I had a night with some friends. You can't exactly blame me, can you? If I'd come home you'd only have nagged for hours about how dreadful I am!'

'Oh, Jeff! That's not fair, dear. It was my duty to try and make you see how terribly you — '

'There you go, you see! I haven't much time so I'd better come to the point. I'm off to Europe, Auntie, with Stepfather Charles!'

'Oh, Jeff. You mean you are with him now? Can I speak with him? Is he . . . '

Jeff moved the receiver away from his ear, letting her words pour into empty air while he blew a kiss at the telephone girl. Aunt Georgie was still talking.

'Isn't he coming to visit?'

'No, Aunt Georgie. He's got to get back to his office right away — tonight, in fact. No, you can't speak with him — he's out right now trying to get plane reservations. No, I haven't got my clothes but I shan't want them — my rich step-pappy can buy me some nice English clothes when we get to London.'

'Oh, Jeff! Then I won't see you before you leave?'

'No, Aunt, you won't. And after all the horrible things you've said to me,' (Jeff grinned to himself, enjoying this) 'no doubt you'll be glad to be seeing the back of me.'

The voice at the other end became tearful, incoherent.

'My poor sister's only child . . . always loved you . . . gave you what you wanted . . . so ashamed with everyone knowing . . . you will write, won't you?'

Jeff began to get impatient. The telephone girl was dealing with another customer and he was getting bored.

'I have to go, Aunt Georgie. All the best!'

'Jeff, don't ring off, dear. I want you to know I still love you . . . '

Deliberately, Jeff replaced the receiver. Aunt Georgie and her unending, all-enduring, all-forgiving love — he was sick of it. It had been far too easy ever since the first day he had gone to live with her, to do whatever he wanted with her. He'd run her life — she hadn't run his — not even when he was six years old. At first he'd been quite fond of her — thought it decent when she'd caught him stealing a dollar bill from her handbag not to whip him. But soon he'd grown to despise her and all the other silly old women who were her friends, who patted his curly head and talked in coy voices and told him he was 'just so handsome!'.

Being irresistible had its drawbacks. It wasn't much fun when there wasn't at least a little resistance to overcome. When he was a few years older, the girls had been as weak as the women, allowing him to do what he wanted with them. The too-easy conquests had begun to pall and he turned his interests elsewhere for thrills — like that last night when he'd said to Hank:

'Bet I can knock up a hundred and twenty in this.'

'Jeff, don't be a fool. You're tight!'

'Jeff, don't. I'm scared!'

'Please, Jeff, I'd rather not!'

Oh, well, one learned one's lesson — he'd do his speeding sober next time.

'Ah, there you are, Jeff. I've booked a room for you and we've reservations for tomorrow's plane. Your aunt quite happy?'

Jeff gave his most charming smile.

'Much relieved, sir, to know that I'm in good hands.'

It was a little too smooth but Charles let it pass. After all, the boy was American, different from the lads at home. At Jeff's age he wouldn't have known how to pay so easy a compliment. The fact was the boy was decent enough at heart, prepared to take the blame and the consequences in order to help a boy less well-off than himself. They must see, Suzanne and he, if they could recompense the lad for his untimely exodus from college. Must have been pretty unpleasant for him.

He put his arm affectionately on Jeff's shoulder and suddenly longed for Rupert to be this age; old enough to enjoy a first-class dinner and to recognise a good bottle of wine.

3

'They may be very pretty but they are a darned sight too expensive!' Murray remarked gloomily in reply to his friend's whistle at a passing bikini-clad French girl.

He rolled over on to his stomach and grimaced at the scratch of the hot sand against his burnt red midriff.

'It's all very well for you, Greg, with your capitalist parents providing you with unlimited pocket money. You can *afford* what just undulated by.'

His friend, Greg Somerville, grinned. He had only known Murray Peters a year and yet they were so well attuned that it seemed now to both boys that they must always have been friends. When holidays had come up for discussion, it had been taken for granted by both that they would holiday together.

'Can't afford it!' had been Murray's comment when Greg suggested the South of France.

'I'll pay!' Greg offered at once, but knew before he'd finished speaking Murray would never agree to this. Murray came from a simple background, working his way through grammar school to win a top scholarship at the same large provincial university where Greg, himself, had just managed to scrounge a place after failing Oxford and Cambridge, which had been his parents' choice, but beyond Greg's ability to achieve. His father was a leading brain specialist and Greg, his only child, had had the best of everything. What Murray found so particularly likeable about him was that despite his privileged upbringing, he was without the smallest trace of snobbery and had sought Murray's friendship quite regardless of their social and financial differences. Of the two, Murray was far more conscious of and affected by them than Greg.

The boys were opposites to look at as well as in temperament. Murray was quiet, clever, studious, but slow in his ability to absorb new ideas, thoughts, methods. He was dark-haired, dark-eyed and thought nothing of his appearance, so that the general effect was usually somewhat dishevelled. Greg sometimes teased him and called him The Professor, but his young, unlined face and bright intelligent eyes prevented the description fitting him too accurately. Perhaps, when he was a good deal older than his eighteen years, the description would really fit him. But not yet.

Greg, fair-haired, blue-eyed, freckled and nearly always laughing, looked much more the eternal schoolboy. His rather mischievous, frank face was open, attractive and already very appealing to the opposite sex. But Greg did not take life or girls or work very seriously. He was content to live on the crest of the wave, enjoying his youth, his sudden freedom from school discipline and intended to make the best of every moment before he was forced to buckle down to work once more when he went to university.

He had been often to the South of France for summer holidays with his parents. He loved water-skiing, bathing and the happy-go-lucky carefree life of the Riviera and wanted his friend Murray to discover the same delights. Murray's holidays had been confined to Southend, Blackpool and, once, to the Cornish Riviera, which Greg told him was not quite the same.

It was Greg who found, as usual, a solution to their differing purses. They would go camping — that was cheap enough and would be fun, too.

They had arrived a week ago — finding a suitable camping site, perfect weather, and the sea a Mediterranean postcard blue and luke-warm, waiting to tempt them into its depths. For two days they had done little else but eat, sleep and swim. Then they had met two French girls on the beach and both boys, sworn to keep to a weekly budget within Murray's means, discovered that in one evening out they had dissipated two whole weeks' allowance.

'No more girls!' Greg said regretfully.

Murray leant on one elbow and looked at his friend with a worried frown.

'See here, Greg, just because I can't afford it, there's no earthly reason why you . . .'

'Cut it out!' Greg said softly but firmly. Then, to ease the moment, he laughed and punched Murray in the biceps and added: 'We'll find somewhere cheaper to pitch the tents. I'm sure there must be a place.' He sat up and hugged his knees, staring out across the hot sand and shimmering sea to a haze on the horizon. 'The chap in the bar was telling me that's an island out there. You can see it properly when it's not buried in this heat haze. It's called L'Isle de la Topaze — Topaz Island. There's no one on it — the owners are English and only come out occasionally when the villa is opened up and servants imported from the main-land to look after them. I was thinking, Murray — suppose we hired a boat and went out there — we could camp for nothing.'

Murray sat up and followed Greg's pointing finger.

'I don't suppose we'd be allowed!' he said with his usual caution and level-headedness. 'It's bound to be private — trespassers heavily prosecuted.'

'I know — but who's to find out we're there if the place is deserted. Let's nip over this afternoon, Murray — we can have a look round and see if it's possible — fresh water — that sort of thing. Could be fun — not a soul there. We can dispense with our clothes — go native. I think I'd like that!'

'I don't know if we should . . . ' Murray began but broke off. Once Greg had an idea, however crazy, he knew it was useless to try to argue him out of it. It was not in Greg's nature to see snags — he was incurably optimistic. Besides, their finances were in a sorry state if they were going to last out till July. Saving the camp site fees would make all the difference — they could even save enough to have a fling their last week . . .

He watched another girl walk past, swinging her hips and looking sideways down at Greg who grinned back at her without the slightest trace of shyness. He wished he had Greg's easy way with girls, but he was still rather shy with the opposite sex — at least with everyone except Betty — the girl next door to whom he was very secretly and unofficially engaged. It would be years and years before he could afford to marry her and yet he knew that one day he would. It made him less girl-conscious than Greg who had no steady girl and shuddered at the thought.

'Marry! Not for decades!' Greg had said. 'I want a good time before I settle down.'

He wondered, for the hundredth time, why Greg liked his company. He seemed to himself so boring compared with his friend.

It had been the merest fluke which had brought them together. Greg's father had treated his ten-year-old sister when she had been knocked down by a motor-bike and lain in hospital in a coma for six interminable weeks. Everyone had expected she would die, but Mr. Somerville had done a miracle operation and Sheila had made a complete recovery. Some months after Sheila had been discharged from hospital, Mr. Somerville and Greg had been driving past the road where the Peters lived and on an impulse had stopped off so that the brain specialist could look up his little patient, to whom he had become very attached. Murray's parents had invited him to stay to tea, Greg had been brought in from the car to join them and despite Mrs. Peters' nervousness at entertaining so illustrious a guest, the tea-party had turned out to be the greatest fun — thanks to Greg and his father who had joked and teased until everyone lost their shyness and was at ease.

It was then the two boys had discovered they were trying for the same local university and Greg had invited Murray to his house and the friendship had begun. Two or three times a week, the boys bussed or biked from one neighbourhood to the other's in order to spend their free time together. They were parted only during term-time because Greg was a boarder at a big public school while Murray, a year younger, was in his last term at the Grammar.

'Wish I had your brain!' Greg would say when he flunked his exams as often as Murray passed with honours.

'Wish I had your games ability!' Murray would retort. He knew that Greg was in all his school teams and had won the shooting cup three years running for his house.

Greg's father was delighted with the friendship. He had not always had money and although Greg had had everything money could buy, he was delighted to see the boy was not growing up a snob or to despise the simple working-class background from which his parents had risen. At one time, he'd half hoped Greg might follow in his footsteps into medicine but he soon discovered his son's nature did not equip him for long years of study. Greg was adventurous, impetuous, too eager to forge his way ahead in the world and be something — the what didn't matter just so long as Greg was active and occupied. His one big flair was for languages and it was this natural ability rather than any hard work that had scraped Greg into university at the third try.

Both parents approved of the boys' plan to go camping together abroad. Murray's family trusted Greg absolutely, because they knew he had often travelled with his parents and would know how to 'cope' in a foreign land; Greg's parents because they knew and liked Murray and considered him the necessary steadying influence for their dashing young son. They would happily have paid for both boys' holiday but admired Murray for refusing their help and Greg for supporting him by agreeing to do the two or three months they planned on a shoestring.

Murray watched his friend staring with a thoughtful expression at the hazy outline of the island. He wondered what he was thinking.

'No girls there!' he commented wryly.

Greg's face broke into a smile.

'No temptations then. Seriously, Murray, the more I think about it, the more fun I think it might be. I gather the place is steeped in ancient history — used to be a pirates' hideout years ago. Then in the last war, the French Resistance used it for smuggling people in and out of the country. There are a lot of rocks and caves and rumour has it that there was once an underground passage from the villa — which is really a château — down to the beach. I can't wait to explore it.'

'Want to play Robinson Crusoe!' Murray teased and received another punch in the ribs. But it was too hot for even friendly fighting and they lay back under the striped umbrella. Greg's face was dreamy again.

'Topaz Island!' he said sleepily. 'Sounds really romantic, doesn't it? Pity we can't take a couple of girls with us!'

'You and your girls!' Murray sighed, but he thought of Betty and the honeymoon they might one day have and how wonderful it would be to take her to a place called Topaz Island where the sun blazed down and the water was ninety degrees and where you could be totally and completely shut off from the rest of the world.

He was nearly asleep when Greg jumped to his feet and announced:

'I'm going to swim and cool off and then I'm going to see about hiring a boat. You coming, layabout?'

'No!' Murray grunted, but Greg took a handful of hot sand and dropped it on to Murray's oily back where it irritated unbearably. With a sigh of resignation, he got to his feet and followed his more energetic companion into the water.

It was five o'clock and several degrees cooler when the smart little motor boat drew up on the silver sand on Topaz Island. Both the boys wore shirts to prevent any further burning but the sun still blazed down on them. They were uncomfortably hot. They sat in the little boat, looking around the beach. On all sides, rocky cliffs surrounded the bay. This, it seemed, was the only landing place. There was a wooden jetty to which they tied the boat but the water looked so inviting, Greg decided to wade ashore. It was crystal clear and because of this its depth was deceptive and the water was soaking the edge of Greg's shorts as he lowered himself over the side. He grimaced and beckoned Murray to join him.

'There's some steps cut into the rocks over there,' he said, pointing to a jagged path cut up the nearly sheer rock face. Murray preferred the jetty which was well built and fairly free of the usual green slime which clung to jetties in England. They reached the path simultaneously and began the steep ascent. Greg was less puffed than Murray when they reached the top and paused to look round them.

'Château! I'll say!' Greg gasped. 'It's more like a Moorish Palace!'

An endless series of paved terraces rose one above the other upwards towards the long beautiful white villa which stood on the highest point of the tiny island. White walls covered with flaming bougainvilia separated each terrace from the next, and terminated in the walls of the villa from which hung a mass of brilliant flowers. The roof was of jade-green tiles which showed startlingly colourful against the cloudless blue brilliance of the sky. Surprisingly, there was a small wood of fir trees to one side of the villa, adding their deeper blue-green to the scene. It was impossible to see what lay beyond the villa for the ground fell away sharply behind it.

'Come on!' Greg said eagerly, beginning to hurry up the flagged pathway which led in a straight upward line through the terraces. 'I can't wait to see the rest!'

In five minutes they were on the same level as the villa itself which was just as impressive at close quarters. There were flower-beds all round the terrace, carefully tended and ablaze with colour.

'Someone must come and see to the place!' Greg commented. 'It's all in apple-pie order!'

He peered inquisitively through a chink in a shuttered window but was unable to see anything. Murray following, he walked round the house. Now, suddenly, the two boys realised why this island had the magical name of Topaz. The natural lie of the rocks had formed a big basin, the size of a small lake. High above sea level, it lay iridescent like a vast jewelled bowl, glittering with all the colours of topaz — light blue, rose pink, straw yellow, dazzling and unbelievably strange.

'But what is it?' Murray said, frowning.

'A swimming pool!' Greg shouted, jumping down the rocks to lean over the edge. 'See, here it is — the pipe which supplies the water. There must be a pump somewhere which pumps water up from sea level.'

'But it's a hundred feet or more!' Murray expostulated.

'Well, the water comes from somewhere!' Greg said carelessly. 'Just think what it must be like when it's full — too beautiful for words. I wonder if there's really topaz in the rocks — enough to make it sparkle like this, I mean. Come on — let's see what else there is.'

Beyond the topaz pool, the rocks became more jagged, covered here and there with a rough thyme-like turf but for the most part bare. There was a breeze now and the air was distinctly cooler. The boys wandered down to a lower level and stopped suddenly at the same moment.

'Hear what I hear?' Greg murmured. 'Water!'

'Must be the sea!' Murray said, his ear to the rocks as he tried to trace the direction from where the sound of running water came. 'Couldn't be a stream or river.'

'A spring?' Greg asked.

'Out here — on an island?' Murray asked doubtfully.

They searched until they found what at first Greg insisted was a spring but when they tasted the water it turned out to be salt. It came bubbling up between the rocks and ran in a deeply grooved bed in the rocks back down to the sea.

'It's fantastic!' Murray said. 'How could the sea come up here!'

'Must be some kind of tunnel and pressure of water from below!' Greg agreed. 'Fascinating. Looks as if we're going to have to bring some fresh water with us. I wonder how they manage at the house.'

'Château!' Murray corrected, smiling.

'Villa!' said Greg. He stood up and stretched himself and suddenly shivered.

'It's getting cool — fantastic how quickly it gets chilly out here.'

'The sun's going down!' Murray said, looking out across the sea. 'It'll be dark soon. We'd better get back!'

Greg nodded.

'Let's just see what's down below!'

'Better not!' Murray cautioned. 'It'll take us quite a while getting back up again. As far as we know there isn't a way round to the beach so we'll have to climb back up this way and go down the terrace way. We can see the rest tomorrow.'

Greg paused. He felt an unaccountable excitement and curiosity to see the rest of the island. He was sorry they hadn't come out here sooner. Now it would all have to wait until tomorrow.

Murray was quite right — it would soon be dark and it was already cool enough to make him wish he had a pullover with him.

They walked back up the rocks, pausing to have a last look at the villa, now mysterious and even more unexpected in the deepening twilight. It was deathly quiet — not even the sound of the crickets which sang so incessantly on the mainland.

'If this were England there'd be sea-gulls!' said Greg.

Dusk had all but taken possession of the beach when at last they reached it once more.

'Can't even see the boat!' Murray grumbled.

'Yes — over there!' Greg said, pointing. Suddenly his hand gripped his friend's arm and he said urgently:

'Murray — look, there's somebody there — bending over the boat — can you see? Look — there!'

'I don't think . . . ' Murray began and then, startling Greg, he shouted, '*Hey*

45

— *you, leave that boat alone!*' He broke free from Greg's hand on his arm and began to run along the jetty. Greg, the faster runner, caught him up and pulled him to a stop.

'Don't be such an idiot!' he breathed in Murray's ear. 'We're trespassers. That might be a caretaker or something.'

'But he was untying the boat, I'm sure of it!' Murray panted uncertainly. 'Can you still see him? Is the boat there?'

'Don't know!' Greg said, his voice a whisper now. 'It's too dark. I suppose we'd better go and make sure that idiot has not let our boat go.'

With the same thought in mind, Murray began to run again but the darkness, soft and velvety but blinding, forced him to a walk, Greg close on his heels. A minute later, they reached the end of the jetty and Murray knelt down and felt for the rope.

'It's gone!' he said. 'I was right!'

'Can't be gone very far!' Greg replied

tautly, and before Murray realised what he intended, Greg was in the water, swimming in ever-widening circles.

He paused, wondering whether to join Greg in the search and decided sensibly that one of them had better stay put. It was now pitch dark and if Greg found the boat he'd need a light to find his way back to the jetty. Murray felt in his shorts pocket and sighed his relief on feeling a box of matches there. He didn't smoke cigarettes but very occasionally, when he was shy or nervous or worried, he smoked a pipe. It made him feel older, more mature and Betty liked it. So he carried it with him — in case he needed it. But it was the matches he needed now. He lit one and heard Greg call out at the same moment.

'Got it! That you, Murray, showing a light? Keep it on, idiot — I can't see you now.'

'It's blown out!' Murray shouted back. 'Hang on, I'll light another.'

47

He did so and heard the sound of the boat engine coughing and then spluttering into life. He lit two more matches before the boat drew into the jetty and Greg said:

'That was a fine carry-on. What the hell was that fool up to, I wonder. And who was it, anyway? God, I'm cold.'

'Here, take this!' Murray said, pulling off his own dry T-shirt. 'I'm not at all cold.'

Greg took it gratefully and a moment later they were heading for the mainland.

'Funny thing!' he said after a minute. 'I mean, if there was a caretaker on the island, why didn't he show himself before? There we were poking round the villa and so on — he must have seen us.'

'And heard us!'

'I suppose there really was someone there? You're sure, Murray?'

'Yes, of course I'm sure,' Murray said at once. 'Didn't you see him? You said . . . '

'I know, I was practically sure but we might have been mistaken. Maybe the boat broke loose — tide changing or something!'

But when they drew up on the mainland, they knew they had not been mistaken after all. The rope was clean cut — moreover it had been cut with a very sharp knife for it was clean and not hacked as it might have been with a penknife.

'And that's odd, too!' Greg said as they walked back to the camping site. 'I mean, why not untie the rope? Why cut it? Mysteriouser and mysteriouser!'

'Yes, and colder and colder!' said Murray, breaking into a trot. 'Come on, Greg, or we shall be catching good old English colds.'

Greg ran beside him, the exercise beginning to warm him now. Five minutes later, they could see the camp lights and they slowed down to a walk.

'One thing is for sure!' said Greg as they went into their tent. 'I'm going back tomorrow to find out who's on that island. Whoever it was, was trespassing.'

Murray grinned.

'So were we!' he said.

4

Darling Granny,

Here I am keeping my promise to write to you a long newsy letter every week. There is so much to tell you I hardly know where to begin. I think I'll start with Jenny because I spend most of my time with her. She is nearly eight and although full of mischief, she is a poppet — full of life and fun and at times, very funny. She tries to be very grown-up and uses long words she doesn't really understand. At the moment she is in bed fast asleep which is surprising as she is so strung up with excitement at the thought of going to Topaz Island next week. She is very like her mother to look at and, as you know, Suzanne is lovely.

I still feel a bit embarrassed calling my employer 'Suzanne' but I'm begin-ning to get used to it. She is so friendly and sweet and treats me like one of the family. All the same, I can't bring myself to call Mr. Kingley 'Charles' although Suzanne keeps telling me to do so. He is miles older than his wife, very distinguished looking, with hair that is going grey at the temples and a fascinating deep very English voice. I like him very much. He came back from New York yesterday and surprised everyone by bringing with him his stepson by his first marriage, a boy called Jeff Aymon. The surname is French because his American mother was married to a Frenchman before she married Mr. Kingley. Jeff is about eighteen and very good-looking and great fun. It's quite impossible to feel shy with him the way I do with Mr. Kingley. Jeff is coming to Topaz Island, too, and we are leaving exactly a week today. Mr. Kingley brought our air tickets back with him last night and Suzanne says we will begin packing tomorrow.

Rupert, the baby, is round and

chubby and no trouble at all. I don't have very much to do with him because Suzanne likes to look after him herself when she can. She says she never had a chance with Jenny because Nanny was an Ogre and wouldn't let her near the nurseries. This arrangement suits us both as I don't know much about babies and I find Jenny easy enough to manage. She does try it on occasionally but always with a twinkle in her eye and I soon have her back under control. Suzanne said yesterday that I manage her very well so I presume I am proving satisfactory.

It really does seem, Granny, as if I've landed the Perfect Job, with a capital P. The house is gorgeous and the food great, and I'm just like one of the family. At dinner last night Mr. Kingley actually teased me about Jeff, telling me to watch my step because he suspected Jeff was a bit of a lad. I wouldn't be a bit surprised because he's so attractive I imagine he must have had girls falling for him right, left and centre in

America. But don't worry, Gran — he's not likely to be interested in me. I'm not nearly sophisticated enough or pretty enough or amusing enough to interest someone like Jeff. He's much older in his ways than you'd expect of an eighteen-year-old English boy — in fact he and Suzanne are more like brother and sister. Jeff was teasing her last night when he called her step-mother though of course, they are not really related at all and Mr. Kingley is only related by his marriage to Jeff's mother.

Suzanne has given me the most lovely dress for France. It's a strawberry pink linen, sleeveless with a boat neck which suits me. It must have cost the earth and looks completely new but Suzanne said she wore it a lot last year and she's tired of it so I can have it. Wasn't it sweet of her! I'm dying to wear it but it's not suitable for this time of year in England so I had to wear the new navy skirt and top last night for dinner. Of course, I mean to save some money for university but I think if I put half my salary into savings I could afford a few more clothes — at any rate, I'm hoping to aim at this although Suzanne says I'm not to buy anything for France until she goes through her wardrobe next week because she thinks she has masses of last year's things she'll want to get rid of. I know she has lots of money and can buy anything she wants but all the same, I'm sure she is just saying she is tired of her clothes because she has seen how few I have. It would be just like her — she's always so kind and generous. She paid for me to go to her own hairdresser last week to have my hair cut and highlighted.

'You'll need something easy to manage in France,' she said, 'because you'll be in and out of the water all day long.' She wouldn't let me pay anything towards it, not even the tip! I think you'd like the way it looks now, Gran — I'm thrilled. It's only a loose, short very simple style — it's the way it has been cut which makes it looks so smart

— hard to describe as it is very casual and yet smart at the same time.

I had to break off my letter there because Jeff knocked on the door to tell me Suzanne had given permission for him to take me out to dinner and a film so I had to down tools and change and rush off. It was a marvellous evening — Jeff is obviously very used to taking girls to smart restaurants and making them feel at ease. I was a bit scared at first, never having wined and dined in the West End, but Jeff told me what to do and I don't think I made any blunders.

Of course, it was probably very dull for him but he said he enjoyed it, too, and that it was a change taking out a girl who was unspoilt. Apparently, American girls are very demanding and want to do all the talking. I was more than happy to sit back and let Jeff talk which he does very amusingly. He paid me a lot of compliments but I think that's just his way — it doesn't mean anything. He wanted me to kiss him *good night, too, and when I refused, told me this was an accepted part of a date where he came from. I felt a bit of a prig but although I like him very much, I couldn't kiss a stranger. Anyway, I don't think Mr. and Mrs. Kingley would want their stepson flirting with the mother's help, do you?*

Time to go to bed, so I'll end this with lots of love, Granny darling. I'll write again next week.

Ever your loving,
Phillida

* * *

A week later, Phil made her third attempt to keep her promise to write another long letter to her grandmother. Suzanne was walking in the park with Rupert and Jenny — usually Phil's afternoon job but there had been some last-minute packing to do and Phil had stayed behind to finish it. Now there was nothing more to be done. She sat down at the writing table in the drawingroom and pulled out a sheet of paper. She had written the date and 'Darling . . .' when a voice from behind her said softly:

'Darling . . . now, I wonder, darling who? Tom? Dick? Harry?'

Phil gasped. She had not heard Jeff come into the room and his sudden appearance and voice behind her made her jump.

'Sorry if I scared you!' Jeff's voice was amused. She felt his hand on her shoulder and twisted round in her chair to look at him.

'Well, you did! And it's rude to read other people's letters!'

His blue eyes looked down into hers laughing.

'So I apologise. But I'm still curious, my pretty Phillida. It would seem that my innocent little English girlfriend is not quite so innocent after all.'

To Phil's annoyance a dark blush spread over her face.

'That's silly!' she said, annoyed with him and herself. 'As a matter of fact,

I'm trying to write to my grandmother.'

'Then stop trying and kiss me instead!'

The blush deepened. Phil felt young and uncertain how to deal with Jeff in this mood. His voice was teasing but she knew that he really did want to kiss her. He'd been trying continually to do so ever since the night she'd gone to the film with him. It was only a game to him, she was sure, but kissing was something she took seriously. Occasionally she had let boys kiss her but she had not enjoyed the experience. She told herself afterwards that it was her own fault for thinking that serious kissing had to be bracketed with love, or something close to love, before it could be enjoyed. It worried her that most of her girlfriends seemed to think and talk of little else and there had even been moments of serious concern that she might be undersexed, frigid.

The pressure of Jeff's hand on her shoulder increased and she trembled nervously. She wished Suzanne and the children were home — Jeff never flirted with her when they were around. Yet at the same time, she half wanted this moment to continue. Jeff was very attractive. If he'd really been interested in her, she might all too easily have fallen for him in a big way. But a sixth sense warned her that Jeff was not in the very least serious. How could he be when she was dull, shy, naïve and inexperienced? She could talk intelligently enough about serious subjects with Mr. Kingley but she couldn't begin to keep up with Jeff when it came to repartee — in fact the light banter was quite beyond her and she felt far more gauche and schoolgirlish in Jeff's presence than in the presence of her elderly employer.

'Jeff, please, I want to finish this letter. We're off first thing in the morning and I promised Granny . . . '

Jeff smiled and moved away from her, swinging his long supple frame into the comfortable sofa.

'So it really is Granny and not

another boyfriend. I'm glad, my pretty Phillida. I'd hate to find I had a rival.'

She felt the best thing was to ignore him and she went back to her letter but could not concentrate. In the background of her thoughts she could hear Jeff singing softly. He had a nice voice and despite herself, she was listening.

'*I want you for my own, yes I do, oh, so much . . .*'

She felt his eyes on her and tried not to look up. She was uneasily conscious of him and they both knew it. Presently Jeff stopped humming and said:

'I think Suzanne is too beautiful for words. I admire her and approve of her but alas, I fear the compliment is not returned.'

This time Phil did look up in surprise.

'Whatever makes you say that, Jeff? I'm sure Suzanne likes you. That day after you arrived she told me herself what fun it was acquiring a grown-up stepson and what fun it would be for us all going to Topaz Island.'

Jeff sighed.

'That, honey, was all of six days ago. Since then she has hardened her heart.'

'But, Jeff, why? I mean, what makes you think so? I'm sure you're wrong!'

Jeff remained silent. He certainly did not intend to tell Phil the real reason — that two nights ago he had one too many of step-papa's brandies and that his goodnight kiss on his pretty stepmother's lips had not exactly been a filial one. Suzanne had been furious and only the timely arrival of step-papa himself had prevented her slapping his face. In the morning he'd spun a tale about being so tight he couldn't even remember going up to bed the night before, but Suzanne had not believed him. At any rate, she'd been very cool and off-hand since. Not that he really gave a damn — he'd known from the beginning that the cool and lovely blonde was not for him, blast it. His stepfather had already won the field and despite the disparity in their ages, they were far too devoted for Suzanne to require consolation elsewhere. No, it would be much more profitable and amusing to seduce the innocent Phillida. She was something quite new to whet his appetite. In the States little girls were out on their first dates at the tender age of ten. By the time they were seventeen they knew all the ropes. Phil was totally inexperienced and refreshingly naïve. Her every emotion showed on that sensitive little face and he knew very well that she found him attractive. It intrigued him that her prim old-fashioned principles had been strong enough to make her resist his attempts to kiss her. Of course, he could have done it by force but then that would have antagonised her and if they were going to spend long months on a deserted island together, he preferred to take his time and let his slow seduction bring its just rewards

'I think . . . ' he said slowly, 'that my stepfather may have been telling tales. I was chucked out of college, you know, that's why I'm here in England.'

Seeing he had Phil's full attention now, he launched into the same story he had told his stepfather. Phillida accepted it without question.

'Surely Mr. Kingley believed you?'

'Apparently not!' Jeff said, sighing deeply. 'He must still have his suspicions and have passed them on to Suzanne. I can't think what else could have made her so distant so suddenly.'

Phil remained silent. She would have liked, for Jeff's sake, to deny the fact that Suzanne *had* been a bit unfriendly towards him. She was reminded suddenly of Suzanne's surprising remark last night when they were upstairs alone together.

'I know Jeff's very attractive, Phil, but don't forget that everything that glitters is not gold. He's a pretty smooth character and I'm not sure you should believe everything he says.'

Phillida had blushed, taking Suzanne's words to mean a warning to her not to be silly enough to fall for Jeff because he wasn't to be trusted.

Almost as if he read her thoughts, Jeff said suddenly:

'I hope you won't let Suzanne put you off me, Phillida. I know you admire her and she is a swell person but you must remember she is a woman — moreover a young woman married to an old man. She's probably jealous of you because you are young and free and because she knows I find you so much more attractive than her.'

'Jeff!' Her voice was shocked. 'That's a horrible thing to say about Suzanne. She's not like that at all. Anyway, Mr. Kingley isn't old . . . and they're very much in love. As to Suzanne being jealous — she's everything I'd like to be, and kind and sweet as well. I won't hear another word against her.'

'Okay, okay!' Jeff's voice was soothing. 'You will take everything so seriously. You didn't think I meant it, did you, Phillida?'

She felt herself blushing again. She *had* thought he meant it. How stupid she was — how childish he must be thinking her.

'Silly little girl!' Jeff's voice was gentle. 'Can't you see that I'm the one who's jealous. Jealous of Mr. Unknown. I just won't believe there isn't a man in your life, hidden away.'

'Well, there isn't!' Phil said. 'I've been far too busy working to think much about boys. I wish you'd stop bringing up this subject.'

'I will, if you'll let me kiss you!'

'I don't want you to kiss me!' Phil replied and at that moment, knew that she did. There was something that fascinated her about Jeff — that made it impossible for her to ignore him; forget him; rebuff him. Perhaps it was that slow, lazy teasing voice; or the smouldering blue eyes; or those long sensitive hands which were always touching her lightly on her hair, her shoulder, her arm with a seeming casualness she could not emulate.

'But you will!' Jeff's voice was softer than ever but she heard him quite clearly. 'Wait for those hot, sultry nights on the romantic Topaz Island; that should stir your cold English heart to warmth — you and me alone in the moonlight with the waves lapping on the golden sand . . . '

'Jeff, I'm trying to write my letter!'

This time he was quiet, but she could no longer think of news to write to her grandmother. Now her mind was filled with the picture Jeff had painted for her and every nerve in her body was alive and tingling. Was it with fear or with excitement, or both? It was with immense relief that she heard Suzanne's voice in the hall and Jenny's piping treble calling:

'Where are you, Phil? We're back.'

'Another chance wasted!' Jeff whispered and gave her a wink as Suzanne and the children walked into the room.

5

Phil lay on the rocks propped up on one elbow so that she could keep an eye on Jenny. The little girl was splashing around the incredible swimming pool supported by a pair of bright blue arm bands. Suzanne was up at the house where Rupert was taking an after-lunch nap. Charles (somehow she still found it difficult to call him anything but Mr. Kingley) was on the mainland ordering supplies. Only Jeff was missing — he'd wandered off after coffee and Phil had no idea where he was.

In a way, she was glad he was not here. He made her nervous and self-conscious; no, more than that! He made her hopelessly aware of herself as a woman and at the same time, aware of him as a man. Suzanne had given her the minute white bikini she was now wearing and insisted that she put it on when she and Jenny decided to have their first swim since their arrival. She'd longed to put it on, knowing how flattering it would be on her young, slim figure but at the same time, she was shy at the thought of revealing so much in front of Jeff's ever-attentive eyes. He would be certain to pay her an extravagant compliment and while one part of her longed to hear it, the other part dreaded it for she knew she would blush and feel young and gauche.

'I must stop thinking about Jeff!' she told herself firmly. 'Suzanne is absolutely right — I mustn't take him so seriously. He's just a natural flirt and the sooner I get used to ignoring him, the better!'

But how could one ignore Jeff? No matter where she was, what she was doing, he was never far away and his extraordinary blue eyes were always fastened on her when she turned and met his gaze.

During the journey out by air yesterday, Jeff had been very efficient and helpful and a model of correct behaviour. He seemed to be perfectly at ease in the confusion of Heathrow and with Mr. Kingley there as well, the whole journey had passed with the maximum ease and comfort. A hired car had driven them from Nice Airport down the coast road and it was Jeff who had taken Rupert, now hot and fretful, on to his knee and kept him amused during the long three-hour drive.

It was teatime when the motor boat brought them across to the island and darkness had fallen so quickly after their landing that when they climbed the beautiful terraces up to the house, it welcomed them with a blaze of lights. There seemed to Phil to be at least a dozen servants — mostly Italian, who came towards them to relieve them of the children, the luggage and to show them up to their rooms.

'We won't bother with the unpacking tonight!' Suzanne said, seeing Phil's pale, tired face. 'Just get the children to bed, Phil dear, and we'll sort everything out tomorrow morning.'

As soon as Jenny and Rupert were tucked up and asleep in the lovely cool bedroom next to her own, Phil had showered and changed into the pink linen dress which was well suited to the twenty-degree rise in temperature since they had left London. Before going downstairs, she had leant out of her bedroom window and tried to make out the contours of the island but there was no moon and she could see nothing but the light at the end of the wooden jetty where the motor boat was tied up. Far beyond she could see a haze of light which she realised came from the coastline.

Tired as she was, excitement gripped her. She had never believed that she would have a chance like this to travel; to live in a foreign country with such a wonderful family on a magical island they actually owned themselves. It was as if she were a different person from the ordinary studious schoolgirl whose only preoccupation was homework and passing exams!

With a little laugh, she had turned from the window and studied her reflection in the mirror. She wasn't the same. The new short hair style, the pink linen model dress, the light touches of make-up she had applied experimentally had produced not a schoolgirl but a young woman.

For the first time in her life, Phil realised that she was pretty. And at once, she needed to be told this was so.

It was, of course, Jeff who told her. They were the first downstairs — Suzanne and Charles were still changing.

'Wow! Can this be my quaint little English girlfriend or is this some lovely island beauty invited to the feast!'

'Oh, Jeff, don't tease!' Phil said, but she'd known his surprise and admiration were genuine and felt the hot colour rush into her cheeks.

After dinner — a magnificent meal with strange foreign dishes Phil had never tasted before but enjoyed — they had coffee on the terrace, lit by ship's lanterns.

'We have our own generator here,' explained Mr. Kingley. 'It was put in after the war. Before that they used oil lamps.'

'And where does the noise of the water come from?' Phil asked. 'It sounds like a waterfall.'

'That's the swimming pool filling up,' explained Suzanne with a smile. 'The water is pumped up from the sea. You'll be able to swim there tomorrow, Phil. It saves walking down to the beach when it's frightfully hot. I won't spoil the surprise by describing the pool to you — it's a natural basin in the rocks.'

Next morning Phil thought it was the most beautiful sight she had ever seen. The water was completely translucent and the incredible colours in the rock face shimmered and glinted in the sunlight like topaz. Now she realised why the island had its name.

'Are you coming in again, Phil?'

Jenny shouted. 'It's super.'

'In a minute!' Phil called back. For the moment she was content to lie here in the marvellous sunshine, feeling it hot and caressing on her bare back. For an instant her eyes closed and in that moment, she felt not just the caress of the sun but a warm hand cupping her smooth shoulder.

'Jeff! You startled me. I never heard you coming!'

He lay down beside her, his eyes now only a few inches from her own, smiling, excited.

'You look gorgeous — you should undress more often. I'd no idea you had such a perfect figure.'

She looked quickly away, excited and yet, as always, afraid. But Jeff put out a hand and tilted her chin so that she was forced once more to look at him. His eyes were not smiling now — they were hot and demanding.

'Kiss me!' he said in a low whisper.

'Jeff, no! Jenny . . . '

'Blast Jenny!' said Jeff violently and

fastened his lips on hers. She drew back at once but not before the touch of his mouth on her own had sent a swift current of feeling right through her body. He tried to pull her back towards him but she jumped up and ran from him, diving beautifully and expertly into the water and swimming with long clean strokes towards the child.

Jeff swore softly. He had been very patient but Phil's shyness was beginning to tantalise him beyond endurance. He knew very well that she found him attractive. Unconscious though it might be, her manner with him was provocative, instinctively so. She was certainly not immune to him. It was high time their 'friendship' developed into something a little more rewarding for him than the sight of her flushed cheeks and downcast eyes. Beside his own purely physical need of a woman — and he had after all not touched a woman in weeks — there was an added stimulant which his recent excursion round the island had given him. He'd discovered several things which were going to make life on the island more than a pleasant holiday and the discovery excited him; made him less cautious with the pretty Phillida because he needed an outlet always for his pent-up emotions. It had always been the same — ever since he was a small boy. A TV play with plenty of fighting and killing and tension could stir in him a violence of feeling that had to be expended somehow; sometimes he would stir up a fight with a boy down the road and punch the younger, weaker boy until the violence was gone out of him. Sometimes he would tease his dog until it snarled at him and then he would beat it, telling his aunt that the dog had attacked him. When he grew older, he would find a girl and take her quickly and brutally. The ones who resisted and whom he could overcome by force gave him the most satisfaction. Unfortunately, girls found him attractive, putting his violence down to passion which they believed they had evoked; putting his callousness down to an indifference he could well afford since every girl in the neighbourhood was simultaneously afraid of and attracted by him and longed to be dated by him.

Afterwards he would be nice to the girls. With his passion and violence spent, he could once more use his brains to gain his own ends. If the girl was frightened and tearful, he would calm her in minutes with protestations of a love so great it had become uncontrollable. This nearly always worked for it flattered and explained his extraordinary behaviour. Later, when he tired of the girl, he would explain that his feelings were so strong that it would be better for them both to part since he was clearly not old enough to marry her.

He felt a moment's fear at the thought of Phillida. At all costs, he must control himself with this one. She could all too easily run to Charles if he stepped out of line and Charles, unfortunately, held the purse strings. Not for the first time, he wondered what had made his American mother tie up her money so securely from her only son. Had she realised that when he grew up, if he could once lay his hands on capital, it would soon be dissipated? Had she guessed his weaknesses even as a small boy of six?

Jeff scowled, remembering his mother without affection. A business woman to the very core; no doubt Charles' English honesty and trustworthiness had seemed an ideal safety deposit for her wealth. Damn Charles — but it wouldn't be for much longer. Somehow, he'd find a way to get hold of the money — big money which would give him not so much the easy life he craved but power. That was what he wanted more than anything in the world — what he meant to get at all costs — power. The pretty Phillida was a very secondary consideration — a momentary pleasure. It was the victory over her quaint old-fashioned principles he

78

wanted; no doubt he'd soon tire of her after he'd seduced her.

He glanced out across the water and saw her slim young body slicing through the rippled surface like a white dolphin. She swam well — gracefully and with an easy rhythm. He could almost feel the suppleness of her body beneath his hands and for a moment desire for her once again overcame caution. He stood up, poised to dive so that he would surface beneath her and hold her for a moment against him — but then a sixth sense made him turn his head and he saw Suzanne standing on the rocks above him, staring down at him. At once, he relaxed and walked towards her with a slow, unhurried stride.

'I've some rather interesting news for you, Suzanne,' he said as he approached her. 'I've discovered a couple of trespassers on the island. I took their names and addresses in case you or Charles wanted to prosecute.'

Suzanne stood perfectly still, fighting her quite inexplicable desire to step back — put distance between her and this young American boy who looked, outwardly, so attractive and yet who unaccountably repelled her. She wondered for a split second before answering him, if she could possibly be pregnant again. That might account for the fact that the boy was getting on her nerves without the slightest reason for doing so. She wished she could explain her feelings to Charles but it was obvious that he'd taken rather a fancy to his stepson and indeed, had no reason not to like him.

'Trespassers?' she repeated, her mind not fully taking in what Jeff had been saying. 'What do you mean?'

'A couple of young English boys — camping in the fir trees down there!' Jeff said, pointing. 'I told them they'd better be off the place by the time Charles got back or they'd be in serious trouble.'

Suzanne edged past Jeff and he

followed her down to the rocks where she seated herself beside Phillida's bathing towel.

'I don't suppose Charles would mind — not if they're boys.'

Jeff looked taken aback.

'Well, I thought it a damned nerve!' Jeff said hotly. 'After all, this is a private island and they've no right to be here. I said . . . '

'It wasn't your business to say anything!' Suzanne broke in quietly. She really wasn't concerned one way or the other about the campers but something in Jeff's manner stung her to take the opposite view to his own. Perhaps it was childish, but she felt glad she was able to annoy him by doing so. Jeff looked like a small boy whose balloon had been pricked.

'You mean, you're going to let them stay?'

Suzanne looked up and for the first time in days met his eyes and smiled. The smile was without warmth.

'Why, yes!' she said coolly. 'There's

plenty of room on the island for two more people.'

'But Charles . . . '

The smile left Suzanne's eyes and her mouth tightened.

'Charles will be perfectly happy to permit them to stay if I wish them to do so,' she interrupted icily. 'Now perhaps you'll tell me just where they are and I'll walk down and see them.'

Jeff's body was now a mass of taut nerves and aching muscles. He was fighting hard to control himself. In his mind, as he watched her walk away from him, he was calling after her, 'Bitch, bitch!' but it didn't help. He had been deliberately squashed and it was a feeling he didn't care for in the least.

Suzanne felt his hot gaze on her back as she walked with deliberate slowness down towards the fir trees. She was trembling but that didn't matter now she knew he couldn't see how that little battle of wills had upset her. It would take some explaining to Charles but she didn't care — she didn't care! The only important thing was that she'd put Jeff Aymon in his place.

The dark shadows beneath the fir trees brought a sudden coolness to her burning cheeks. The dry pine needles pricked her feet in the Cleopatra sandals. Not very far off, she could hear voices. She called out:

'Hullo? Whereabouts are you?'

A few minutes later, the two boys appeared from her left-hand side and approached her awkwardly.

'I say, I'm afraid we aren't packed up yet!' said Greg apologetically. 'The gear takes a bit of stowing . . . '

'I came to tell you it was all right — you can stay!' Suzanne broke in. The young men stood staring down at her at first in surprise and then with bright, warm smiles. She smiled back at them, liking their English faces, their eager boys' voices as they both started to thank her at once.

'We were brewing a cuppa!' Murray said at last shyly. 'Would you like to come and have one with us?'

Suzanne nodded and Greg took her arm — not intimately, as Jeff would have done, but politely, to guide her through the trees to the minute clearing where they had pitched their small tent.

'Of course, we knew we were trespassing!' Greg said presently when Suzanne was seated on an upturned box and the boys were sprawled on the pine needles at her feet. 'But we weren't doing any damage and we thought the island was deserted.'

'And we really couldn't afford the campsite fees on the mainland,' Murray finished. 'We're awfully sorry!'

Until the moment of meeting Suzanne, neither had been in the least sorry. The tall superior American boy who had told them to get off the island and quick, had put their backs up and although they knew they'd have to go, they'd been taking as long as possible to get packed. But Suzanne, such a pretty, charming and friendly woman, had made them both anxious to atone — or at least to explain that they hadn't

84

meant any harm to the island property.

'It can't be very comfortable here!' Suzanne said, glancing at the tent and the sleeping-bags rolled up outside it. 'Why not move into the house? We'd be pleased to have you both and there's masses of room, not to mention bathrooms. I should imagine you could do with some mosquito nets, too!'

She smiled as Murray scratched at some ugly red bumps on his bare legs.

'They seem to prefer Murray's lifeblood to mine!' Greg said, grinning. 'That's a very generous offer but I don't think we should impose on you like that. After all . . .'

'After all, why not?' Suzanne broke in. 'Let's introduce ourselves — I'm Suzanne Kingley. My husband, Charles, is over on the mainland getting supplies. I also have with me my daughter, Jennifer, and my baby son, Rupert, and a very charming girl called Phillida Bethel, who is my mother's help. Then there's my stepson, Jeff Aymon . . . but of course you met him earlier, didn't you?'

The boys nodded, neither wishing to tell this charming hospitable woman that they had heartily disliked Jeff Aymon on sight.

Greg said quickly:

'This is my friend, Murray Peters. He's eighteen. I'm nineteen and my name is Greg Somerville. We're both students — due to start at university in October but eking out a summer holiday before we put our backs into our studies.'

Suzanne looked at them, knowing her first instinct was right. They were nice boys and she was not in the least regretful of her impulsive offer to have them to stay.

'Phillida's going to university in October, too,' she told them. 'You'll like her, I know. Tell me, how long have you been here?'

'A week!' Greg said, grinning. 'The place was absolutely deserted until yesterday. We saw you all arrive last night. As a matter of fact, you very nearly caught us on the beach — we were diving off the jetty when Murray heard the boat. Of course, as soon as we saw you we realised you were the owners. We were idiots not to realise you'd be arriving, as they opened up the house two days ago and a boat load of people arrived — presumably staff or something.'

'I said we ought to push off right away but Greg wanted to see you first!' Murray broke off, suddenly shy. Suzanne laughed.

'Well, why not?' said Greg. 'It's such an incredible place, isn't it? I just had to know what kind of people owned it and if you fitted my mental picture of you.'

'Well, do I?' Suzanne asked.

Greg's face was suddenly serious.

'As a matter of fact, you don't — not in the very least.'

Suzanne looked at him curiously. Greg was looking now at his friend and she saw the darker boy nod almost imperceptibly.

'What's all the mystery?' she asked.

Greg sat up and took a deep breath.

'Well, we thought the owner must be some kind of hermit or crank — or something. I mean, ordinary people don't keep caretakers with knives and guns who creep about in the dark.'

'Don't *what?*' said Suzanne, wondering suddenly if Greg was mad. But a glance at his face told her he was perfectly sane and just as puzzled as she was.

'You might as well tell Mrs. Kingley!' said Murray. 'After all, if she is the owner, she ought to know what's going on.'

'Indeed I should!' Suzanne said. 'We don't, as it happens, have a caretaker on the island although we do have an arrangement with some friends on the mainland to send over their gardeners once a month to tidy the place up. What *is* all this about knives and guns?'

'We don't know ourselves what's going on,' said Greg. 'As a matter of fact, I hoped you could explain — that's one of the reasons I wanted to stay on and see you for myself. Look,

I'll tell you what we do know. The first time we came over here — to see if the island was okay to live on — we thought we saw someone on the jetty at dusk. When we ran down the terrace onto the jetty, we found our boat had been set adrift. The rope had been clean cut right through. So someone was on the island — and that someone had a pretty sharp knife, too. The odd thing was, there was no other boat except ours — so whoever it was must have been living on the island — or else he'd got a boat in a cave in one of the rocks.'

'We've been looking all week,' Murray said. 'Every day we've swum a bit further round the island — just to see if we could find a cave or inlet which would take a boat, but no luck so far.'

'And the gun?' Suzanne asked.

'Well, that's even odder. The night we pitched camp we heard two gun shots. The first we weren't sure about as it seemed to come from some way off and we thought maybe it was from the mainland and that the echo had somehow carried across the water. But the second — well, there was no doubt about that — it came from the island.'

Suzanne looked at both boys searchingly.

'You're quite sure? This isn't a . . . a joke, or something?'

The boys shook their heads. She'd known already from their expressions that they were in earnest.

'I must tell my husband . . . no, you must!' she said. 'There certainly ought not to be anyone on the island. You've not heard or seen anything since?'

'Only one thing!' Murray said. 'It rained our third night here and next morning, Greg and I found footprints on the beach. At first we thought they were our own but they couldn't have been — you see, on the left foot of this person, the little toe is missing.'

'I don't know why, but that makes it all sound rather sinister!' said Suzanne, shivering. 'Now I'm more than ever sure you should both come up to the house. It mightn't be safe for you here.'

The boys smiled, self-confident and unafraid.

'We're all right!' Greg said. 'There's two of us and we're pretty sure there's only one of him.'

'Well, I'll still be glad to have you staying with us,' Suzanne said again. 'With two small children in the house I don't like the idea of a prowler — especially one with a knife and a gun. I expect Charles will want to search the island.'

'We've made a pretty thorough search this last week,' Greg said, standing up. 'Fact is, we haven't found a thing. Still, we'd be glad to help your husband have another look.'

'Then it's agreed you'll move up to the house,' Suzanne said, holding out her hand as if to seal a bargain. 'I'll expect you in time for drinks — about six? That'll give me time to explain the whole thing to my husband after he gets home.'

'And what about . . . the American boy?' Murray asked. 'I . . . I don't think he particularly liked us and we don't want to spoil your holiday by being . . .'

'You won't. Jeff is just a visitor, too!' Suzanne said. 'He'll naturally welcome anyone my husband and I care to invite.'

A few moments later she left them and Greg turned to Murray.

'Well! One thing's certain — she doesn't like her stepson any better than we do!' he said. 'Not that I have any sympathy for him. I think she's lovely.'

'So do I!' said Murray. 'Come on — let's get on with the packing. I can't wait to get up there and see the Yank's face when he finds that far from being turfed off the island in disgrace, we're going to be guests of honour in the house.'

Greg grinned.

'Put his nose out of joint, won't it!'

'I'll put yours out of joint if you don't

give me a hand with this tent!' said Murray.

They forgot Jeff and Suzanne as, with occasional bursts of horseplay, they got down to packing up their belongings.

6

To Suzanne's surprise, Jeff was putting himself out to be both polite and friendly to the two English boys. She found herself more than ever puzzled by this American stepson of Charles'. Her own inexplicable mistrust of him seemed quite absurd when he behaved as he was doing this evening, keeping the two boys and Phil in animated conversation and making them all laugh with his wild tales of life on an American campus.

She felt that she ought to like him — and yet during that brief moment by the pool when she had countermanded him over turning the two trespassers off the island, she could have sworn that she had seen an icy hatred in Jeff's eyes — a look which had momentarily frightened her. Now she was asking herself if she had imagined it.

Phil, too, was completely charmed by Jeff's manner. He had sounded furious earlier in the afternoon when he'd told her that Suzanne was permitting two strangers to remain on 'their' island; but since meeting the boys, he seemed to have forgotten his annoyance and was putting himself out to play the perfect host to them. For the one moment they had had to talk to each other privately as they were going in to dinner, she had asked him why he minded the two English boys staying.

'Welcome two rivals for my fair Phillida's hand?' Jeff had replied in a low, intimate voice. 'Of course I wasn't pleased — but they seem reasonable fellows — if a trifle dull!'

Phil didn't find either of the boys 'dull' although it was true that Murray was a bit shy at first and only began to converse easily after dinner. But Greg was a very easy conversationalist and from the first had seemed to fit in agreeably with everyone, Charles, Suzanne and herself, as if he had known them all for years.

Charles Kingley, she was sure, liked both boys very much. He was also very interested in their account of the 'intruder'.

'The past history of the island shows that it has been used as a base for smuggling on a number of occasions,' he told them. 'It is possible that something of the kind is going on again. Tomorrow, if you boys agree, we'll search the island thoroughly. I can't say I like the idea of strangers snooping around when Suzanne and the children and Phillida are here.'

Whilst he engaged Greg in planning tomorrow's search Phillida took the opportunity of studying the boy. He was nice-looking — not as good-looking as Jeff but there was something very open and attractive in his face. She liked the way his eyes crinkled when he laughed, which was often. He was very tanned — unlike his poor friend, Murray, who had been burnt a dark angry red by the sun. Greg's skin was a beautiful golden brown which made his blue eyes even bluer.

Because the two boys had been camping and had not expected to be at all social, they had travelled light, packing only jeans and T-shirts. Jeff, in a very American cream-coloured suit, made the two boys seem younger, less sophisticated, although they were, in fact, all about the same age.

Greg looked up suddenly and caught Phil's eyes on him and for a brief moment their gaze held. Then Greg smiled and she smiled back and it was as if they had said a private 'Hullo!' to one another.

Phil looked down quickly, her usual shyness overtaking her, but at the same time, she felt curiously happy. There was none of that uneasiness she felt when Jeff looked into her eyes — a complicated mixture of thrill and fear. She felt that she could be friends with Greg in a way she could never be just friends with Jeff. Then Jeff said at her elbow:

'A penny for them, or are they worth more? You're very deep in thought!'

She felt the colour rushing into her cheeks which always seemed to happen now when Jeff spoke to her. She hoped self-consciously that no one else in the room noticed how easily she blushed. It was a schoolgirl habit she would give a great deal to be rid of.

'Well?'

'Oh, nothing, Jeff. I was just day-dreaming. The sun has made me sleepy!'

To her relief Murray broke in, discussing the climate and the enervating effect the combination of sun and salt air had given him when they had first arrived.

'But you get used to it after a few days,' he added. 'Then you feel you can tackle anything.'

Jeff said abruptly:

'I never feel tired. I was thinking I might take a walk right now. How about you, Phillida? It's much cooler out — should be swell.'

'I don't think that's a good idea,' Suzanne broke in sharply, then pulled herself up, speaking more calmly. 'I mean, if there really is someone on the island, it might not be safe for Phil to be out in the dark.'

Phil felt rather than saw Jeff stiffen beside her.

'I reckon I could take care of anything that might happen,' he began, but Charles Kingley broke in:

'Phillida's tired anyway, Jeff, so don't try and talk her into it. You don't particularly want a walk, do you, Phillida?'

She shook her head, glad to be given an excuse not to go out alone with Jeff. It was not the walk she objected to but the thought of what Jeff might do and say alone in the dark. He would certainly try to kiss her and somehow she did not want him to.

Then Greg said:

'I noticed a rather beautiful Steinway in that other room. Does anyone play?'

'Suzanne does!' said her husband.

'Very nicely, too.'

'Won't you play for us?' Greg asked his hostess. 'I'd love to hear you.'

Suzanne stood up and flexed her fingers.

'I'm a bit out of practice, but I'll try if you'd really like some music. I don't play pop, I'm afraid — only classical.'

She looked very beautiful as she walked across the room. Her husband stood up and went with her, throwing wide the double doors that led from the *salon* where they were having coffee, into the big room opening out on to the terrace where they had dined.

Jeff walked restlessly over to the window on the opposite side of the room and looked down the almost sheer rock face to the dark sea far below. Only the white crests of the waves were visible for there was no moon as yet. He was trying once more to keep his temper under control. No one in the room knew what it had cost him in will power to be so pleasant tonight. He had not forgiven Suzanne for deliberately countermanding his orders to the English boys to get off the island. Nor could he rid himself of the aggravation of Greg Somerville's presence. What he had said playfully to Phillida about being jealous of Greg was all too true. Phillida did not *seem* particularly smitten with her fellow-countryman, but Jeff could see for himself that Greg was nice-looking, amusing, easy to get on with and with the kind of personality that could easily attract an inexperienced girl like Phillida.

Now, on top of this, Suzanne had baulked him again of his chance to get Phillida alone for a little while. The tendons in his legs and arms throbbed with the tension of a furious anger he was fighting hard not to show. He was not used to being thwarted in any way. What he wanted, he expected to get, if not at once, then very soon afterwards. It was weeks now since he had set out to seduce Phillida and the way things were going, it looked as if he would have even less chance than before of making any headway. Those two boys would be hanging round, getting in the way every time he was able to snatch a few moments alone with her when she was rid of that child who clung to her all day long. And if it wasn't Jenny, it was Suzanne, calling Phil into her bedroom to discuss clothes or hairstyles or something equally stupid. Phillida was practically never alone and he was rapidly coming to the conclusion that this state of affairs was deliberate on Suzanne's part.

While Jeff stood glowering with his back to them Greg moved over and sat down on the sofa beside Phillida. From the next room, the first sweet notes of the well-known aria from *La Bohème* came floating through to them. Greg leant back and sighed contentedly.

'Mrs. Kingley plays beautifully!' he said softly. 'Do you like music, Phillida?'

The girl smiled.

'You must call me Phil — everyone

does as a rule, even Jenny!'

Greg smiled back at her.

'This is from *La Bohème* — one of my favourite operas. Have you seen it?'

Suddenly Phil found herself telling Greg about her life at home with her grandmother — of the unavoidable restrictions caused simply by lack of money. For this reason, she had never been to a concert except once with a school party; never been to the opera or the ballet or even to the theatre. Her only chance to educate herself musically was via the television set.

'I agree that's second best to a live performance,' Greg said at once. 'But in a way, it's rather fun for you because you've got everything to discover for the first time. I'll never forget the first opera I went to — it was *Madame Butterfly* and I was about fifteen. I think it was the most exciting moment of my life. My mother's musical, you see, and although I haven't inherited any talent for performing, I love to listen. But I won't talk or you can't hear

Mrs. Kingley play. Listen to this, Phil — it's really lovely.'

Phil relaxed, leaning back against the soft cushions, her eyes closed, letting the beautiful notes of the piano seep into her consciousness, carrying her away on a wave of sadness and longing and beauty which she did not understand and yet which she felt in the very core of her being. Occasionally Greg's soft voice would penetrate her concentration, telling her the name of the music Suzanne was playing now; perhaps briefly explaining the name of the composer or the part of the opera so that she would understand the story behind the music.

Unknown to Phil, Greg sat watching her face. Not only did it seem beautiful to him, but highly sensitive. As the mood of the music changed, so did her expression. She 'felt' music just as he did. The thought made him curiously happy. Had he stopped to analyse his emotions, he would have known that he was falling in love with this unusual girl. But Greg was not one for self-analysis. He took life very much as he found it, happily, enthusiastically and simply. His relationships with his friends were never complicated and he liked and was liked by most people with whom he came in contact.

He had never fallen in love. The kind of girl he'd met had been very much like himself — amusing, light-hearted and fun to be with. He'd imagined himself in love for a few days at a time and then some other girl would take his fancy and the first one was forgotten. Murray teased him, calling him a 'flirt', but it was simply that his heart had not yet been fully engaged with any girl.

But Phillida held an unusual fascination for him. It was not just that he found her attractive — he'd known prettier girls by far. It was that she was so different from the others. There was nothing hard about her — her looks, her voice, her movements were all gentle and fluid and essentially feminine. There was an old-fashioned element which intrigued him — as if the close association with her elderly grandmother had produced a young Victorian maiden in the middle of the twentieth century. She roused in him all the essentially male desires — to protect, to idolise, to instruct, to cherish — feelings he had not known before with past girlfriends who considered themselves his equal in most things and for whom sex seemed their predominant interest.

When Suzanne came back into the room, her arm linked through her husband's, she said laughing:

'Why, I think I've sent you to sleep, Phil dear!'

Phil opened her eyes wide and said:

'Oh, no, Suzanne — I was listening to every note. It was brilliant! I loved it all.'

'Where's Jeff gone?' Charles asked, looking round the room.

'He muttered something about having his walk anyway and went out about twenty minutes ago,' Murray said.

Neither Greg nor Phil had noticed. Greg said:

'Do you know, Mrs. Kingley, that that was Phil's first introduction to live music. You play beautifully. You did like it, didn't you, Phil?'

'Oh, yes, I did. I'd like to hear it all over again!'

'Well, not tonight!' Suzanne said. 'I'm off to bed. If you children would like a hot drink — or maybe a beer or a coke or something, help yourselves. You'll find what you want in the fridge. I expect the kitchen staff have gone to bed.'

Greg and Murray jumped up and held out their hands in turn, thanking their host and hostess with simple good manners. Phil hesitated, wondering whether she, too, should go to bed, but Suzanne, seeing her hesitate, said:

'There's no need to hurry off to bed if you aren't tired, Phil. But don't be too late up.'

'She is nice!' Murray commented when Suzanne and her husband had left the room. 'I bet she's nice to work for.'

'Marvellous!' Phil agreed. 'I don't feel as if I'm an employee at all. Suzanne treats me like a daughter. I don't think anyone could have a more wonderful job than this.'

'It's such a fantastic place — this island!' Greg said. 'We've had a great week here, although I must confess it'll be nice to sleep in a bed again. As for that bath — that was almost too much of a luxury!' He laughed, stretching his arms above his head and said: 'I suppose the Kingleys have masses of money but they aren't a bit snobby with it. I like them both very much. Tell me, Phil — what about the stepson, Jeff. I can't quite make him out.'

It was a simple question but it caught Phil unprepared and to her acute annoyance she felt herself blushing again.

'Oh, he . . . he's all right!' she stammered.

The blush had not gone unnoticed by

Greg who felt suddenly strangely deflated.

So that's the way it is! he thought. And then Phil resurrected his good mood by adding:

'To tell you the truth, I can't quite make him out, either. Sometimes he's charming and other times . . . well, he frightens me somehow. I don't know why!'

'He's Mr. Kingley's son, I suppose, by an earlier marriage?'

'Well, no — they aren't actually related.' Phil explained the relationship. 'That's why he doesn't look at all like Mr. Kingley.'

'Well, holler any time you need help!' Greg said lightly, but meaning his words in all seriousness. Just let that Yank bother Phil or frighten her when he, Greg, was around and the sparks would fly . . .

'Oh, he's always very nice to me!' Phil said quickly. 'I mean, I shouldn't have said that about being frightened of him. I don't mean it.'

'Well, I could understand it if you were,' Murray broke in unexpectedly. 'You should have heard him when he barged in on our camp. None of the old charm then, was there, Greg? He fairly let fly. Of course, we thought he was the owner so we took it all on the chin and apologised profusely for trespassing. If I'd known he wasn't even a real relation of the owners, I'd have given him back a few words.'

Greg stayed silent. He wasn't sure yet what Phil felt for the American. She had been quick enough to defend him and she blushed every time his name was mentioned. Probably the chap had been making a pass at her and she wasn't sure of her own feelings. If that was the case, there was hope for him . . .

He stopped his thoughts abruptly. Hope for him for what? Was he really interested in her himself? The realisation that he was, kept him unusually quiet and thoughtful. He left Murray to do the talking and studied Phil

110

unobtrusively. Surely, he told himself, it wasn't possible to fall in love during the space of an evening? Personally, he didn't believe in all that twaddle in books about love at first sight. And yet — yet this girl had evoked in him feelings he'd never had for any other girl. His reactions to her were utterly different. With anyone else he would by now be making a pass at her — possibly making a date for the next day, letting her know he was interested, attracted. With Phil, he was doing none of these things. He was just watching her, listening to her, getting to know her and liking her better each moment. Perhaps most of all, he liked her sudden unexpected laughter. She did not laugh often; her manner was serious and rather like that of a little girl allowed to stay up for a grown-up party and on her best behaviour. But underneath there lurked a sense of humour and when she smiled her whole face lit up and the laughter round her mouth and eyes came bubbling up from within her. She was laughing now at Murray's account of their first amateurish attempts to set up camp.

'Phil, Phillida!' He said her name under his breath and felt a curious light-headedness as if her name had by itself the power to intoxicate him.

At that moment, she turned her head and looked at him. Her eyes were still full of laughter but it died slowly as she saw him staring at her. For a long moment they sat looking at one another and then Phil said:

'I think it's time I went up to bed. Good night, Greg! Goodnight, Murray. I'll see you in the morning!'

But it was really to Greg she was talking and her words seemed to him to be a promise — as if she were telling him that this parting wasn't important because they would soon be together again.

Later, pretending to be asleep so Murray would not interrupt his thoughts of her with talk, Greg asked himself if he were imagining the whole episode. Was Phil interested in him? Or had she divided her time and attention equally between him and Murray? Was she just being equally polite to them both, her heart already ensnared by Jeff Aymon?

Greg tossed and turned and could not sleep. He blamed the unaccustomed softness of a bed to sleep in instead of the hard groundsheet he had become used to. He blamed the heat and then the rich three-course dinner. He was too inexperienced in love to know that this alone was his complaint and that Phillida, too, was lying wide-eyed and wakeful in the room above his own.

⋆　⋆　⋆

Over a mile away, Jeff stood in the entrance of a dark cave and shone his torch on the sleeping figure. Gone was his anger of a few hours ago. Now there was only excitement and triumph that he had discovered what he was looking for — and a bonus discovery thrown in.

He had been quite a small boy when his aunt had given him the wooden box that had once belonged to his French father. He had known of its existence ever since his mother's death when the solicitor had handed it to his aunt, saying:

'The boy might like this when he's a little older.'

For two years his aunt had refused point-blank, and with most unusual strength of will, to let him have the box. But on his twelfth birthday, she had been unable to withstand the pressure of his will on hers and she had handed the box over with the key. She, too, had been curious to see what was inside but a simple honesty had prevented her from opening something which belonged solely to her nephew. Now it was her turn to plead with him — that he should open it in front of her and show her the contents.

But Jeff had taken the box up to his bedroom and locked himself in and ignored her hurt, puzzled voice calling after him on the landing outside.

The box had not been a disappoint-ment. In it were all the answers to his past — why his mother would avoid Jeff's questions about his father; why when she had spoken of him her voice was cold and hard and disparaging. His father, though only just old enough to have been in the war, had apparently been a collaborator — no, worse than that; *he had been a traitor!*

Jeff had felt a strange thrill of combined disgust and admiration. Though his father had lacked any feeling of patriotism, he must, Jeff surmised, have had courage and a ruthlessness which found its echo in his own heart. Jacques Aymon had joined the Resistance when the Germans invaded his country. He had worked with them long enough to discover a great deal about them, and then he had betrayed them slowly and in small groups, to the Gestapo.

The Germans had paid him well. Jeff found a notebook in the false bottom of the box which must have escaped even his mother's eyes, a notebook neatly and precisely listing vast sums of money deposited in an Argentinian bank to his father's credit. His double life had gone on for the remainder of the war. No one, apparently, had ever realised that he was betraying his countrymen. Perhaps his father had killed the members of the Gestapo who could have betrayed him to the Allies after the war was over. Jacques Aymon had gone to the Argentine, claimed his by then considerable fortune and taken it to America. There he had married almost at once an American woman with money of her own.

The true horror of what his father had been never disturbed his son. Jeff thought about him only as extremely clever. It made him laugh to discover in the box a medal from de Gaulle for his father's part in the Resistance. He'd taken huge risks — and got away with it.

It was a pity, thought the young Jeff, that his father had not lived a bit longer

— at least long enough to realise that he, Jeff, understood and approved of what he had done. Then, perhaps, his father would have made him his heir instead of leaving his ill-gotten gains to his American wife.

Also in the box was a map. The map was of Topaz Island which had belonged to a distant branch of his father's family. Jeff was not sure quite how the title deeds had come into his father's possession. When he was older he wondered whether his father had had that branch of his family liquidated by the Gestapo in order to acquire the deeds. In any event, they had passed eventually to his mother and then to Charles Kingley. But Jeff had the map and realised that he was probably the only person still alive who knew where to find the secret passage from the villa down to the caves of the east shore of the island, the cave and passage that had been used in centuries gone by for smuggling; for escaping aristocrats in the French Revolution; for contraband;

for every kind of illegal purpose. Jeff supposed this was the reason why his father had wanted the island so badly. He had foreseen the possibilities of making money — just as Jeff had seen them. But never until now had the chance to take advantage of his knowledge come his way.

This morning, the day after their arrival, he had found the passage leading from the cellars down to the cave. So over-hung was the cave mouth by rocks that it could never be seen by a boat circling the island and only by a minute yard-by-yard search of the rocks themselves. But of just as great interest to Jeff was his next discovery — of tightly wire-banded boxes piled on a ledge inside the cave — evidence of someone living there. There was an inflatable rubber dinghy and wooden paddle.

Jeff had had only a moment in which to see all this before he heard a man's cough. He had quickly retired up the steep rock steps of the passage to the cellar. He had no wish to meet the intruder until he had marshalled his thoughts and decided how best to make use of his discoveries. He wanted to know just what was in the boxes — their value; their destination. There were all kinds of exciting possibilities open to him — blackmail; a cut of the profits — for this was clearly some form of smuggling; the most likely being drugs.

Now he was back with, as he had hoped, his man at a complete disadvantage. From what the English boys had said, Jeff knew the intruder had a gun and a knife and might use both. It was safe to assume that whatever he was hiding in the cave was of some value. Jeff longed to open one of the cases but knew he must not risk making a noise. If the man woke, he could get to his gun before Jeff — who had no weapon — was close enough to prevent his use of it.

He took three steps nearer, fixed his eyes on the outstretched hands, and then with his foot kicked the sleeping man.

7

After breakfast, Charles Kingley brought out a large sheet of paper and spread it on the table.

'This,' he announced, 'is a rough map of the island which I have drawn and marked off into sections. If we are going to search the place thoroughly, it might as well be done in an organised way.'

He looked round the table and smiled.

'I know it seems rather improbable on this glorious sunny morning that anything sinister can be going on, but we might as well make quite sure — then we can relax and enjoy our holiday.'

Phil nodded with the others. Mr. Kingley was quite right — it was impossible to feel that anything menaced the peace of this beautiful place. It was still quite early, and there was a wonderful freshness to the air which would be gone by midday when the sun was at its height. The water in the swimming pool sparkled and glinted back its myriad colours. High above, the brilliant Mediterranean blue sky was completely cloudless. Far down below, the sea was a deep blue green, unbroken except where it splashed lazily over the rocky edges of the island. Magnificent, gaily coloured butterflies were dancing in dozens round the bougainvilia and other flowering shrubs that tumbled over the terraces.

Suzanne broke in with a question:

'Would you like to go with the search-party, Phil? I'll manage Jenny and Rupert.'

Phil hesitated. Part of her longed for the adventure the search promised but she did not want to impose on Suzanne's kindness. She was not here for fun but to work.

'Of course she wants to go!' Mr. Kingley broke in with a kindly smile. 'I think we should split up into pairs. I've

121

already told Mario — he's the head gardener, that I want him along, so with Antonio and Sebastian, the houseboys, that makes four couples. We can each search a quarter of the island . . . '

He traced the boundary lines with his finger and the three boys nodded.

'We've already covered most of that ground, sir,' Greg said. 'But the guy — if there is one — could be moving around. We never managed more than a small part of the island at a time. If he was watching out for us, he could have slipped off somewhere else and we wouldn't have run into him.'

'Right, then I suggest as you know the terrain pretty well, you and Murray split up. Murray, you could join Jeff; Greg, you take Phillida and I'll go with Mario. I really don't think we need go armed but a stout stick might not come amiss if there should be any trouble. Yes, Jeff?'

The American boy was staring at his stepfather with a barely concealed look of annoyance.

'I don't think it's right that Phil should be in on this. After all, if there is a rumpus, it's a helluva risk for a girl . . . '

'But I doubt very much we'll find anyone,' his stepfather broke in. 'I'm not doubting the boys saw footprints or that someone cut their boat adrift but I cannot believe anyone is actually living here on the island. And even if 'he' is, there may be some perfectly innocent explanation.' He smiled suddenly at the two English boys. 'After all, you two were here when you should not have been and yet you weren't up to any harm.'

'Well, let Phil pair off with me,' Jeff said. 'As a matter of fact, I've a small pistol upstairs — I could take that with me and then if anything did happen, I can see Phil's okay.'

Charles Kingley frowned.

'I didn't know you had a gun, Jeff. Have you a licence to carry one? I don't like guns lying about the house. You never know when there'll be an accident of some kind.'

'Oh, it's a toy, really!' Jeff said lightly. 'My aunt kept it to scare off burglars — it really can't do much damage.'

'All the same, no guns,' said Charles after a moment's hesitation.

Suzanne broke in now, her face expressionless.

'I'm quite sure Phil will be perfectly safe with Greg. Now, shouldn't you all get started if you're going to be back for lunch?'

Ten minutes later they were on their way. For a brief while Greg was silent and then he said:

'My God, Phil, did you see Jeff Aymon's face just now when Mrs. Kingley said you were to come with me? He looked as if he'd kill her there and then. Phew, I wouldn't much care to come up against him on a dark night!'

Phil frowned. She had not looked at Jeff for she had realised at once that he resented the fact that he wasn't going to be allowed to partner her that morning, and the thought made her self-conscious. It had been something of a relief when Suzanne had unexpectedly settled the argument — a relief, too, to know that she would not be alone with Jeff. All the same, Greg's remark was disturbing. She had known for some time that Jeff's politeness to Suzanne was purely superficial and that, in fact, he disliked her. She could not understand why. Suzanne was always so sweet to everyone and so attractive, too.

'I think the feeling's mutual!' Greg went on. 'I don't think Mrs. Kingley likes him any better than he likes her. Do you know why, Phil?'

'No, I don't!' Phil replied truthfully. 'Anyway, I'm sure you must have imagined a lot of it. I expect Jeff was just . . . ' She broke off shyly but Greg finished the sentence for her.

'Jealous because you were detailed to come with me! Oh, well, if that's the case, I don't blame the poor guy. I'd have been jealous if you'd been going with him.'

With complete naturalness, he gave her a friendly hug.

She felt suddenly radiantly happy. Greg was nice — exceptionally so. He was fun, too, and so very easy to get along with. A lot of her shyness and self-consciousness disappeared with him.

They scrambled over some rocks and approached the small fir wood where Greg and Murray had been camping.

'Like to see where we were?' Greg asked, grinning. 'It wasn't a bad spot — but a bit mosquito-y. Poor old Murray got bitten to pieces but they left me fairly well unscathed — can't taste as nice.'

Laughing, they ran through the trees and came to the small clearing where the tent had been pitched.

Greg stared round him and said thoughtfully:

'Hardly seems possible that this time yesterday I didn't even know you existed. I feel as if I've known you for years!'

Phil smiled back at him.

'Me, too. I'm so glad Suzanne invited you to stay with us.'

'So'm I!' agreed Greg. 'And I think I know why she did — to spite Jeff. Oh, well, who cares about the reason. It's a fabulous villa, isn't it. They're obviously loaded. Perhaps that's what's eating Jeff. I suppose if Mr. Kingley hadn't married again, Jeff would be his heir. Now I imagine young Rupert comes into the family fortune.'

'Well, it's really Jeff's money — in a way,' Phil explained. 'His mother left hers to Mr. Kingley and Jeff only gets the interest on the capital. I'm not quite sure what that means but Jeff told me a bit about it and it seems to amount to the fact that Mr. Kingley has control of the money.'

But Greg was not listening. He was staring down at the ground with a frown on his forehead and a puzzled expression in his eyes.

'That's very odd. Come over here and look, Phil. See this damp patch

127

here? That's where we emptied our jerry-can of water when we broke camp yesterday evening. Now look at this — it's part of a footprint, and I'll swear it isn't Murray's or mine.' His voice rose excitedly. 'Someone else has been here, Phil. Murray and I were both wearing espadrilles. This man was wearing rubber soles of some kind — see the ridges?'

Phil felt an answering excitement mingled with fear.

'Then there really *is* someone else on the island?' she asked.

Greg nodded.

'Unless Jeff or one of the servants came walking down this way last night. You're not scared, Phil?'

She shivered involuntarily and at once he grinned and came close to her, putting an arm round her shoulders.

'Silly! I'll look after you. Would you like to go back and join Mrs. Kingley?'

A moment ago Phil might have said yes, but now, with Greg's warm strong young arm around her, the fear was gone and there remained only the excitement.

'No, I'll stay with you!' she said breathlessly.

Greg gave her a little hug of pleasure.

'Good girl! Come on, let's get the wood searched and then we can be out in the sunshine again. It won't seem nearly so spooky in the sunlight.'

She was glad that he kept hold of her hand. They searched the small wood thoroughly but found nothing else suspicious. Half an hour later, they were out on the far side of the wood, climbing down the rocks towards the sea. The heat of the sun had increased and Phil felt its warmth through the thin white cotton shirt she wore over a pair of yellow linen shorts Suzanne had given her. Her arms and legs were bare and there were only thonged sandals on her feet.

Greg, too, was in shorts — old faded cut-off jeans and a pale blue towelling shirt which he proceeded to strip off with relief.

'I wonder if we can take time off for a swim!' he said, looking longingly at the water below them.

'I don't suppose it would matter 'taking time off',' said Phil. 'But we haven't got our swimming gear.'

Greg laughed. 'We'll swim nude!' He saw the colour rush into Phil's cheeks and said gently: 'You needn't be shy with me, Phil. We can each undress behind a rock and get into the water without looking at each other. I'll promise not to cheat if you do, too!'

In a moment, her shyness was gone.

'All right, but you'd better keep your word, Greg.'

They climbed down to within a few feet of the sea. The rocks, obviously the result of a cliff fall, lay like huge boulders at the water's edge. Greg looked around him and said:

'There you are — you can go behind that one — it's right on the edge. I'll go over there. Race you in, Phil.'

As she stripped off her shirt, shorts and briefs Phil thought:

130

'This can't be me — swimming naked in the sea with a boy I've not even known for twenty-four hours!'

But there was no time for further thought. There was a loud splash on the far side of the rock now strewn with her clothes; and Greg's voice called:

'Come on, slowcoach — it's *wonderful*!'

She dived into the water, prepared for the shock of its coldness and found that it was luke-warm. At once, she relaxed and swam easily out to sea. A few yards behind her, Greg called:

'It's perfect, isn't it? Murray and I always did this before breakfast.'

For a few minutes longer Phil worried about her nakedness. The water was so clear — it was possible to see down to the sea bed. Supposing Greg came closer and could see her . . . Then as suddenly, her modesty vanished. What if he could? She had a lovely body — it was nothing to be ashamed of, and Greg clearly took this as right and natural. It was the first time she had ever swum in the nude and it felt quite perfect. She gave herself up to the simple enjoyment of it.

Greg stayed some distance away. He wanted to swim near to her but sensed that she would be ill at ease if he did. One couldn't expect a girl brought up in so old-fashioned a way as Phil to take to swimming in the nude as readily as he did! Besides, it was one thing to swim naked with Murray and quite another with a girl who attracted you as much as Phil attracted him. He didn't want anything to spoil this friendship that was growing so quickly and pleasantly between them.

Drying themselves was little problem, for the sun was now hot enough to steam the water off them almost as soon as they clambered out. Phil dressed quickly and sat on the top of her rock, her arms hunched round her knees, her short hair lying damp and curly and still dripping on to her glowing cheeks.

'Okay?' Greg asked, joining her.

'It was perfect!' Phil breathed. 'I'm so glad you suggested it, Greg. I'd never have dared on my own.'

'It's really the best way to swim!' Greg said, sitting down beside her. 'Look, borrow my handkerchief to dry your hair. It's a lovely colour! Just like honey.'

He took a strand and rubbed at it with his handkerchief.

Phil felt suddenly shy again. She was not used to compliments — except from her grandmother and that was quite different!

'Now you're blushing again!' Greg said, laughing. 'I'm sorry if I've embarrassed you. You mustn't take any notice of me. I always speak before I think.'

He sounded so apologetic, Phil said truthfully:

'I don't mind — honestly. It's just — well, I'm not used to going out alone with boys — I expect you think I'm really stupid.'

'No, I don't!' Greg said seriously. 'As

a matter of fact, I think you're absolutely sweet — and now I've made you blush again. Perhaps it would be easier if you could think of me as a kind of brother — hell, no. That's the last thing I want. Anyway, that's made you smile. You've a lovely smile — it lights up your whole face, as if someone inside you had lit a torch.'

'Sounds horribly ghostly to me!' Phil laughed.

Greg stood up.

'Talking of ghosts reminds me we are supposed to be looking for one. I hate to say it, but we'd better get a move on.'

He held out his hand and pulled her to her feet.

Phil's sandals slipped on the damp rock and she slid towards Greg who put out his arms to save her. Quite suddenly she was in his arms and they were staring into one another's eyes. Phil's heart began a furious, unsteady beating. It was not unlike the curious feeling she had had when Jeff kissed her only now there was only sunlight reflected in Greg's blue eyes, and a feeling of intense happiness.

Then Greg's lips were against hers and for a moment, time stood still.

With an effort, Greg stopped kissing her.

'I'm sorry!' he said, fighting to get control of himself again. Somehow that kiss had been quite unlike any kiss he had given any other girl. And Phillida had kissed him back — that was the incredible thing. 'It happened so suddenly . . .'

This time it was Phil putting him at ease.

'I didn't mind. I . . . please *don't* be sorry, Greg.' She gave a sudden impish grin which made him want to kiss her again.

'You're okay!' said Greg, linking his arm through hers. 'I feel really good — happy. Do you feel happy, too?'

Phil nodded — her heart was too full for words. Madness it might be, but she was falling in love for the first time in her life; in love with a boy she had only just met and yet whom she already seemed to have known for half a lifetime. What on earth, she wondered, would her grandmother say if she knew how she had behaved this morning? It would have shocked her, but Phil was sure this was all right. Greg liked her — he'd made that clear enough and she was falling in love with him. Maybe there was some magic about this island which altered time so that an hour could be a year or a second. The sunlight and beauty were so romantic and intoxicating that normal behaviour seemed strange and the strange quite normal.

Then Greg said:

'I wonder if there really *is* someone on the island actually hiding from us? If he is hiding, then he's up to no good. I think we've got to accept that there's *someone*. I wonder if the others have found any clues.'

At once the mood of the moment was gone and Phil remembered that the island might be dangerous as well as romantic; that all was not quite perfect after all. There was Jeff, too. He would not like it when he found out how much she was attracted to Greg. She must try not to let it show — especially in front of the others.

'Look, there's Mr. Kingley and the gardener. Let's call them and find out if they've seen anything.'

'Only this!' said Charles Kingley when they joined him a few moments later. He held out a fairly new pair of wire cutters. 'Mario says there are none missing in the tool shed. There was only one pair anyway and he used them last night when he noticed that one of the creepers was falling against a shutter on the house.'

'I fixa it late, Signor — then I take the cutters and locka my shed as I allways do the same. See, I have here the key.'

Greg mentioned the footprint and it was decided that they should go back to the villa to see if the other two couples had found anything. The two Italian houseboys had not yet returned but Murray and Jeff were drinking cokes beside the pool.

'Not a thing!' Jeff said in answer to his stepfather's question.

Murray said:

'Of course, we didn't actually swim out round the rocks — to see if there were any caves or anything. Jeff didn't think there was much point doing so.'

'Well, no!' agreed Charles. 'We can go right round the island by boat — might do that after lunch. Let's all have a swim now and cool off.'

'You look as if you've been in already, Phillida!'

Jeff's voice was cold — almost accusing. Phil's hand went instinctively to her still-wet hair and the colour began to mount in her cheeks.

Greg saved her. He said:

'She had a dip in the sea, didn't you, Phil? I was put on my Boy Scout's honour not to watch!'

'And I hope you can be trusted!' said Charles Kingley, laughing.

Phil stole a quick look at Greg's hair and saw with relief that it had already dried. There was nothing to show that he, too, had been swimming. Jeff must have come to this conclusion, too, for he said more quickly:

'We used to do a lot of nude swimming in the States — it can be fun. Coming in again, Phil?'

She hesitated. Instinct warned her not to make an enemy of Jeff and yet she had not the slightest wish to be 'appropriated' by him. His voice was almost possessive — as if she belonged to him. Involuntarily, she shivered and Suzanne, watching them, said:

'Would you mind awfully not swimming just for a bit, Phil? I put Rupert down for his nap a little while ago and he was rather restless. I think maybe the sudden heat is upsetting him.'

'Oh, of course, I'll go up now and have a look at him,' Phil said, wondering for the second time that day if Suzanne had deliberately stepped in to her rescue.

Five minutes later, she knew that this was so. Suzanne followed her up to the house and met her as she came out of Rupert's room. The little boy was fast asleep.

Suzanne smiled.

'I told a white lie just now, Phil. Rupert went off to sleep like a lamb. Forgive me if I did the wrong thing but I had the idea you didn't want to go into the pool just then.'

She linked her arm through Phil's and led the way into her own bedroom. She sat down at the dressing table and began to uncoil her long fair hair.

'Thank you!' Phil said simply. 'I told a white lie, too — at least, I let Greg infer one. As a matter of fact, we both swam. It . . . it was wonderful!'

Suzanne turned and looked at Phillida's flushed face and then she smiled.

'You like Greg, don't you? So do I! I think he's a boy you can trust. Just as I know without asking that I can trust you. Now if it had been Jeff . . . ' She broke off, her face dark and unhappy.

'Suzanne, you don't like Jeff, do you? Why?'

'Do you like him?' Suzanne asked sharply. Phil caught her breath.

'I don't know. He's . . . he's attractive, and yet . . . he frightens me. I don't know why.'

'Well, that's just how I feel about him!' Suzanne said, turning back to her mirror and beginning to wind up her hair slowly and methodically. 'And men can say what they like about 'a woman's instinct' but I'll back it every time. My instinct warns me *against* Jeff. Now that I know yours does, too, I'm even more sure he isn't to be trusted. He's too attractive. Charles doesn't see it, of course. Jeff is always impeccably correct with my husband and he takes him at face value.'

'Jeff can be good fun.'

'Look, Phil, you're very young and I promised your grandmother I would take the greatest care of you. I know you aren't used to taking care of yourself — at least, not with boys. I'd be a lot easier in my mind if you would promise to keep Jeff at a distance. I know that isn't physically possible with him part of the family, but you know what I mean. Don't let him think you find him attractive.'

'But I don't . . . I mean, I can see with my eyes that he is attractive but he doesn't attract me. I much prefer . . . '

'Greg? Then that's wonderful. I'm more than glad I asked those two boys to stay. I like them both. I expect you'll think I'm very overcautious but as a matter of fact, I put a telephone call through to Greg's parents this morning — just to check their story. After all, apart from you to be looked after, there is also Jenny and Rupert and the boys were complete strangers. I thought it as well to be quite sure about them. Anyway, I need not have worried — once again my instinct was right and the boys are just what we thought them. There's just one thing, Phil — Greg's father says he's a bit of a madcap and they are never quite sure what he'll be up to next. I'm quite sure nothing Greg could do would be *really* wrong but it does sound as if he's a bit impulsive. It's highly possible that he'll fall for you — but you mustn't take it too seriously if he does. From what his father said about him, it's a different girl every week! I don't want you to get hurt, Phil.'

'Of course not — I wouldn't take him seriously,' Phil said quickly, but something inside her cried out against Suzanne's warning. The friendship was very new — very precarious and uncertain in its embryonic state and yet already it had become important to her; already she *had* taken Greg's interest in her seriously. It was too late to take back that kiss which, however lightly given on Greg's part, had woken something in her which she had never known before.

'Anyway,' she added defensively, 'I don't see why you think Greg should be interested in me.'

143

'Because,' said Suzanne, smiling, 'you are a very unusual girl. You may not know it but you are about as different from the modern girl as it is possible to be. You are one hundred per cent feminine, very pretty and very innocent. That combination is quite irresistible to the discerning male. I'm only sorry that it should be proving irresistible to Jeff, too. You will be careful of him, won't you?'

'Anyone would think,' said Phil with an effort, 'that poor Jeff was as dangerous as the mysterious intruder! Greg is sure 'he' exists.'

'Even if 'he' does, I'm much more afraid of Jeff,' said Suzanne more to herself than to Phil. 'Somehow I have the most awful feeling that he and not the intruder is where the danger lies.'

She stood up and sighed and gave Phil a quick smile.

'I expect I'm being over-imaginative. Charles says I am. He thinks Jeff is just a spoilt boy. Perhaps he is. Now, let's forget him.'

'It must be lunchtime,' Phil said. 'I'll go and get Jenny.'

Suzanne nodded and Phil went back downstairs, her face thoughtful and clouded with apprehension. Suzanne had inadvertently passed on to her a new and stronger fear of Jeff.

8

All day long, Jeff tried to get Phil on her
own, but she stayed by the swimming
pool with the children, and Murray and
Greg, turned down his suggestions of a
walk down to the beach or a ride over
to the mainland in the motor boat.
Suzanne's warnings about Jeff had
made Phil determined to make Jeff
understand once and for all that she
wasn't in the least interested in him.
She hoped that when he saw how much
she liked Greg and Murray, he would
realise that it was useless trying to
attract her attention to himself, and
leave her alone.

Jeff, however, was not put off so
easily. His chance came when Charles
decided to run Suzanne over to the
mainland after tea to visit some friends
who were staying in a large hotel near
by. By half past six, Phil had put both

Jenny and Rupert to bed and Greg and Murray had gone off to the woods to see if they could find any fresh traces of the 'intruder'.

Jeff stopped Phil on the landing as she came out of the children's nursery. His face was flushed and his eyes were blazing with an excitement that seemed to fit his words.

'I've just seen a man down by the jetty!' he told her in a low voice so that the children should not hear. 'I know it isn't Greg or Murray because the guy I saw was wearing long trousers and the boys were in shorts. It could be the intruder, Phillida. I think we should go take a look.'

Phil hesitated. She had promised Suzanne she would not leave the children alone in the house while they were out. At the same time, Charles Kingley had been most anxious that if anyone saw anything in the least suspicious, they should investigate immediately. She hesitated.

Jeff, watching her face, said:

'I'd go on my own but we'd sure have more chance of catching him if there are two of us after him. If we see him again, you could run back here and bring the boys along to help me while I trailed him.'

Phil saw the sense of this. If Jeff ran back for help, he might lose sight of the man, and if they waited till Greg and Murray came back from their walk, the intruder would have plenty of time to disappear.

'Come on, Phil!' Jeff said, taking her arm. 'The kids'll be okay — you can tell the maid to keep an ear out for them.'

For a moment longer, Phil hesitated. Then one of the Italian maids came out of Suzanne's room where she had been turning down the beds and Jeff at once called to her, explaining that she was to stay in the children's nursery until Phillida returned.

Phil was excited and afraid at the same time. She had never really fully believed in the 'intruder', especially since the day they had all searched the island so thoroughly and found nothing. But now Jeff had actually *seen* him. It never occurred to her that this might be a ruse to get her on her own. Jeff sounded and looked completely convincing.

She followed him down the path through the terraces, glad that he offered to go first and hoping that she was not going to be weak enough to let Jeff see how scared she was. They reached the jetty and stared round them, but the little beach and surrounding rocks seemed deserted. Jeff shrugged his shoulders.

'He can't be far away — it isn't five minutes since I saw him. Let's see if we can find footprints in the sand.'

Phil pulled the cardigan she had flung over her shoulders closer round her bare arms. There was the usual drop in temperature now that the sun was almost gone and she suddenly shivered. In half an hour it would be quite dark.

Jeff studied the beach and turned back to her.

'Not a thing!' he said, shrugging his shoulders. 'I suppose he was too crafty to lay a trail for us to follow him. He must have gone over the rocks. Let's go take a look.'

Phil followed him across the sand on to the rocks. It was possible by climbing a little way, to edge round beneath the cliff that semicircled the little bay. Jeff was ahead of her, moving out in a seawards direction, keeping close under the cliff face. Phil scrambled after him, not wanting to have too much distance between them. The water in the rock pools was lukewarm. Occasionally, a small crab would scurry out of her way. Ahead of her, Jeff paused and held up something.

'Found a clue!' he called to her. But he didn't say what it was and she saw him fling the object out to sea. She wondered why he'd not kept it to show his stepfather later but had no time to ponder the oddity as Jeff was beckoning her to follow him.

When she finally caught up with him, they had travelled right round the cliff and were on the edge of the adjoining bay. Suddenly Phil recognised it as the place where she and Greg had bathed.

Jeff, startlingly close to her ear, said curiously:

'Seen anything, Phil?'

'No!' She didn't want to talk to Jeff about that morning — somehow it was private and special to her and Greg. After the swim they had searched this part of the island thoroughly and seen nothing suspicious. 'I don't think we're going to find anything here,' she added. 'Let's go back, Jeff.'

He put an arm round her shoulders and felt her stiffen at his touch.

'You're not frightened with me here to look after you, honey?'

'No, I'm not frightened!' Phil said. 'I just think this search useless; whoever it is has had long enough to hide. Besides, I don't think I should have left the children even though Maria is there.

Suzanne might not like it.'

Jeff's arm was still around her and she moved just far enough away to get out of his reach. But at once, he caught hold of her hand and said urgently:

'I think it's me you're frightened of, Phillida. You jump like a grasshopper when I touch you. Why are you so scared? You must know by now that I'm crazy about you. I've been darned patient up till now — surely I'm entitled to some little reward?'

Phil felt the tell-tale colour rush to her face. She bit her lip nervously. This was the kind of conversation she found so embarrassing.

'Jeff, we're down here to look for the intruder. If we're going to stay then surely we'd best forget everything else and go on searching.'

She tried to move away but Jeff swung her round by her arm so that they stood opposite one another. His face was against what little light there was left in the sky and looked to the girl dark and menacing.

'Let me go, Jeff, *please*!'

Ignoring her plea, he took her forcibly in his arms and began to kiss her. Phil closed her mouth tightly, clenching her teeth and fists and twisting her head from side to side to avoid Jeff's kisses. She was now really frightened. Jeff was no longer just flirting with her — teasing her. His fingers were digging into the soft flesh of her arms and his mouth was bruising her lips so that she cried out in pain. For a moment, his kissing stopped and she heard him give a low, husky laugh. Then his mouth was on hers again and she felt her legs giving way as he forced her backwards on to the rocks.

Fiercely and with all the strength she could muster, she fought to free herself but he was far stronger — stronger even than he appeared, and seemed not even to notice when she kicked him hard against his knee with her sandalled foot.

'You're mine!' he said against her mouth. 'Mine, mine, mine, and I'm going to have you, Phillida.'

As he moved his hand to touch her body, she felt his grip slacken and brought up her arm to hit him as hard as she could across the face. He moved back for an instant with surprise and pain and in that moment, she swung sideways and picked up a loose piece of rock.

'If you touch me again, I'll hit you — with this!' she cried.

Jeff knelt back on his heels and, shockingly, he laughed.

'You're quite the little spitfire when you're angry, aren't you? I'd no idea that beneath the little-girl façade lurked a woman of passion.'

'Don't you dare touch me!' Phil gasped. 'I'll tell Suzanne and you'll be sent away.'

To her intense surprise, Jeff's expression of amusement gave way to one of uncertainty. Phil's pleas for mercy couldn't have moved him one iota from his desire, but this chance threat struck home. Suzanne would indeed send him packing! And that was the very last thing he wanted. Crazy not to have thought of it — but he'd been so sure that once he started to make love to her, Phil would have succumbed like all the others.

He stood up and stared down at her, his eyes glittering with an emotion she could not guess at.

'What a nasty little tease you are!' he said brutally. 'You lead me on, pretending you want me as much as I want you, and then you turn round and threaten me.'

Phil sat up, her eyes enormous, her face now chalk white and quivering.

'That's not fair. I never wanted you. I never let you think I did. I don't even *like* you!'

'But you found me attractive!' Jeff said scornfully. 'I'm not an inexperienced idiot, Phillida. Don't tell me that when I took you out in London you weren't attracted. You wanted me to kiss you — though you played the little innocent.'

Phillida felt as if she was living in a

nightmare. Jeff's last words shocked her — they were too near the truth. At the beginning, she had indeed found Jeff attractive — she'd written and told Granny so in those very words! *Was she a tease?* Without in the least meaning to, had she led him on to imagine that she wanted — *this?*

She shuddered.

'I'm sorry if I let you think I . . . that . . . I'm sorry if it was my fault. But now at least you know the truth. I wish you *would* leave the island. I wish you hadn't come here in the first place!'

Jeff's eyes narrowed.

'Oh, yes, I can understand that. You've changed your tune since you came here, haven't you. It's that Greg Somerville you've got your eye on now. That's why you've lost interest in me — found someone more to your taste and . . . '

'Stop it, Jeff!' Now her fear had given way to anger. 'I'll admit I like Greg — and his friend — better than I like you, but I don't see that it is any of your business. I'm free to like whom I choose.'

'Just you go on thinking that!' Jeff replied, his voice now suddenly lowered to a tone more vicious than taunting. 'You'll find out that I'm right. *You're going to belong to me, Phillida.* There'll be a way — you'll see.'

Frightened though she was, Phil faced him, her chin high.

'Are you threatening me?' she asked. Despite herself, her voice was trembling.

'Not threatening — just promising!' Jeff retorted. 'And don't go carrying tales to Suzanne. A girl who is willing to bathe in the nude with a complete stranger looking on is hardly as innocent as she'd like to make out. In fact, I think Suzanne could be made to believe that it was your idea that we came down here.'

'That's absurd!' Phil flashed back. 'She knows already that Greg and I . . . anyway, she doesn't like you, she warned me about you. She'd take my word sooner than yours.'

Jeff shrugged.

'Maybe! I'm not so sure your boyfriend would. Greg doesn't really know you very well, does he? A carelessly spoken word by me could make him think twice about you.'

Phil was suddenly too disgusted to go on listening. Apparently Jeff had no scruples at all — he was every bit as nasty as she and Suzanne had felt intuitively but, until now, without just cause.

She gave him a look of utter loathing and with deliberate casualness turned back in the direction of the villa. There was no sound of Jeff following her and after a few minutes, she turned round but could see no sign of him. At the same time, the sun disappeared between the sea and the sky and it was suddenly pitch dark.

She stumbled in her haste to get back to the villa and grazed her knee badly on a jagged rock. Tears came into her eyes that were partly from the pain but also from the reaction of the horrible scene with Jeff. She was having to feel her way now — the line of the beach was only very faintly discernible a hundred yards ahead of her. Twice more she fell. Each time she got to her feet, she turned to see if Jeff was following and breathed a sigh of relief that there was no dark shadow behind her. She remembered the intruder and suddenly wondered if Jeff really had seen someone by the jetty or if it had been a ruse to get her away from the house. She could now no longer stop the tears that flowed silently down her cheeks.

Somehow, the distance between her and the shore lessened and suddenly she could see the outline of the wooden jetty. She stumbled over the last of the rocks and half fell on the warm sand. High above her rose the terraces and above them the marvellously welcome lights of the villa.

She lay for a moment recovering her breath and then stood up. As she did so, two dark shadows sprang at her from the level of the first terrace. She felt their combined weight hit her, then the wind was knocked from her and with a shuddering gasp she fell once more on to the sand.

9

She recovered her breath and with it returned the horrifying fear of those two dark shapes hurtling towards her. As she opened her mouth to scream, she heard a voice beside her saying:

'Great Scott, it's Phil. Greg, get up, you idiot, it's *Phil*!'

Then the two intruders materialised into Murray and Greg and Phil lay quietly, looking up at them with relief, surprise, amazement and an hysterical desire to laugh and cry at the same time.

Greg was kneeling beside her, smoothing the sand off her face with hands that were wonderfully gentle as he poured out apologies.

'Phil, we thought you were the intruder! Murray and I heard someone coming across the rocks as we were returning from our walk; we decided to hide up on the terrace behind the wall and ambush whoever it was as they went by below us. Oh, Phil, you poor kid. You're not badly hurt, are you? This is *awful*!'

'I'm all right!' Phil gasped out. 'I just feel a bit sick. *I* thought *you* were the intruders . . . you gave me such a fright.'

Murray had lit a match and was holding it up in the darkness.

'Your knees are bleeding!' he said anxiously. 'I say, Greg, we did hurt her. We were doing a flying rugger tackle . . . gosh, I'm sorry!'

Phil gave a deep sigh of relief. After all that had happened, their voices and words were so blessedly normal. She sat up and was suddenly conscious of Greg's arm around her. She leant back against his warm comforting shoulder and felt better. She began to explain how she and Jeff had gone round the cliff in search of someone Jeff had seen prowling on the beach.

'Where is Jeff now, then?' Murray

162

asked after she'd told them how she'd slipped on her way back in the dark. 'Did he find anything? Were you coming for help?'

'Hold on!' Greg interrupted Murray's eager questions. 'Poor old Phil probably isn't feeling like an inquisition. I think we'd better carry her back up to the house.'

'Oh, no, I'll be all right!' Phil said. 'Really, I'm much better. I think you just winded me.' She paused, longing to tell the boys what had really happened out there on the rocks — to get it off her mind. But Jeff's warning still rang strongly in her ears. He just might tell Greg that a rendezvous with him in the dark was her idea, and Greg might believe him. She couldn't bear the thought that Greg might do so. He'd be so disgusted. His good opinion of her was strangely important to her. She dare not risk it. So she said:

'Jeff stayed for a last look around but as it was getting dark I came back. I was worried about leaving the children.'

She began to struggle to her feet and the boys were eager to help her. Each took an arm and they half carried her up the steep path to the villa. Despite her pronouncement that she was all right, her legs would not stop trembling and the grazes on her knees stung with the sand and salt from her fall when the boys had 'attacked' her. She was more than grateful for their support. She just wished she did not feel like crying every time they said kind and encouraging things to her.

At the villa, Greg took charge. He sent for Maria, who assured them both children were perfectly all right, then told her to put hot bottles in Phil's bed and run her a hot bath.

Murray was despatched to the kitchen to tell the cook to make tea.

'You're suffering from shock!' Greg told her firmly. 'I've seen enough unfortunate victims brought to my father's surgery after road accidents and the like — that's why you're trembling and shivering. You get into bed as quickly as you can, Phil. I'll come up and see you and you can tell me all about it then. Murray can go and see if Jeff needs any help.'

As he spoke, he was guiding her upstairs. Giddiness had now added to the sick feeling in her stomach. She was only too pleased to let Greg look after her in this way and take all responsibility off her shoulders.

Although at first the effort of having a bath when she felt so weak seemed too much, when she stepped out of the hot water she was miraculously better. The cuts on her legs still stung but they were clean of sand and were less sore. As she dried herself, she saw that some big bruises had come up on her arms and realised that Jeff and not the rocks had caused them. She shuddered and hurried into her dressing-gown and into her warm bed.

It was Greg who came in with the tray of tea. He put it down on the bedside table and sat himself down beside her.

'It's supposed to be tea but it's almost too weak to do you much good. Anyway, put lots of sugar in it — that's what's important. How're you feeling?'

She smiled back at him.

'Miles better!' It wasn't enough to describe just how much better she felt — not only physically but because Greg was there, so normal and nice and trustworthy. The menace of Jeff's violent, angry face receded into the back of her mind like a bad dream.

'Murray and I never thought *you'd* be down on the beach at this time of night. We knew it couldn't be Suzanne or Charles as we saw them go off in the boat. I suppose we might have considered it could be Jeff but . . . ' He broke off, looking suddenly much younger and very self-conscious.

'But what?' Phillida asked, curious to know his reasoning.

Greg shrugged, as if he had made up his mind to speak out no matter what. He said:

'Well, Murray did suggest it could be

Jeff but I said as you were alone in the villa, Jeff would certainly be hanging around somewhere near.'

He saw Phillida's cheeks burning with colour and looked down at his feet unhappily.

'You like him, don't you, Phil?'

Phil swallowed nervously.

'No, I don't. I don't know why you should think so. I . . . I try to avoid him as much as possible.'

'Well, I suppose that's why I thought there was something between you.' Greg looked up and grinned. 'I wondered if you were just pretending to avoid him because you were afraid we'd all guess how you really felt; that was why you set out to behave in public as if he didn't mean a thing. Don't you really like him?'

'*No, I don't!*' Her voice was so vehement, there was no doubting it. Greg said shrewdly:

'But *he's* fallen for *you*. I've seen the way he looks at you.'

'Well, I wish he wouldn't!' Phil said.

'Oh, don't let's talk about Jeff, Greg. I'd rather not.'

Greg nodded, smiling.

'That suits me. To be honest, I've been a bit jealous, not that I've any right, of course, but, well . . . I suppose I felt he had an unfair advantage. I mean, that week in London before I even knew you. Do you mind me talking like this?'

Phil was too honest to pretend that Greg's faltering words were making her anything but extremely happy. But they also made her feel very shy. Greg, however, was not intending to take the matter any further for the moment. It was enough to know that Phil liked him — and that she wasn't even half-way in love with Jeff. He breathed a big sigh of relief and said:

'I wonder how old Murray's making out . . . if they've found anyone. I can't think why someone should be hiding on the island — not unless they're smuggling or drug running! Be rather fun if we found him and his loot and got rich overnight on the reward some grateful government ought to offer us!'

'You are an idiot!' Phil said, laughing. '*I* don't believe there is anyone — at least, I don't *think* so, though I'll admit I did when you and Murray sprang out of the dark at me. I was dead scared.'

'You were brave about it afterwards!' Greg said warmly. 'I think you're a good sport, Phil, as well as being the prettiest girl I know. By the way, how are the knees?'

'A bit sore — but I put some antiseptic ointment on them — I'm sure they'll be okay tomorrow.'

Greg's face darkened.

'I don't think Jeff should have allowed you to come back on your own across those rocks. Suppose that man he saw had been hiding this side of the cliff — why, you might really have been attacked, Phil.'

Phil giggled.

'Well, I was attacked — by you and Murray!'

'No, seriously!' Greg said. 'Jeff ought

to have had more sense. Incidentally he and Murray *are* being an age. I wonder . . . '

He was interrupted by a knock on the door. It was Murray, still holding his torch and looking mystified.

'Just couldn't see a sign of Jeff!' he announced. 'I went right across that adjoining bay, too, hollering and shouting but there wasn't sight nor sound of anyone. I hope he's okay.'

'Serve him right if the intruder has knocked him out!' Greg said unconcerned. 'He'd no right to leave Phil to come back alone in the dark . . . *and* it was stupid of him to go off alone like that.'

'All the same,' Murray protested. 'I think perhaps we ought to do something, Greg. Suppose he's really been injured — we can't leave him lying out all night.'

Greg stood up, sighing.

'I suppose not — though it's crazy really. You've searched that part of the island and he might be anywhere by now. What can *we* do with two small torches? We need a ruddy searchlight to see anyone lying amongst those boulders.'

'The moon's coming up. In ten minutes or so we ought to be able to see fairly well.'

'Right — then we'll eat first and go look for him after, if he still isn't back. How's that?' Greg asked.

'You all right now, Phil?' Murray asked shyly.

'Well enough to be feeling hungry!' Phil said, smiling.

Greg glanced at his watch.

'Seven-thirty — dinner-time. I'll go and ask Maria to send you up a tray. We'll send word if Jeff turns up and if he hasn't, we'll come back after we've searched the island. See you later, Phil.'

When the boys had gone, Phil lay back on her pillows suddenly very tired. The combination of sun, sea air and so much emotional tension was too much even for her young metabolism. She tried not to remember that horrible ten minutes with Jeff. In retrospect, she found it hard to believe that he had really intended to assault her. She wondered now if she had imagined a lot of what happened; if perhaps Jeff's behaviour had been passionate rather than violent. After all, he *had* left her alone in the end.

She searched her conscience, trying to remember any incident in the past when she had encouraged Jeff, however inadvertently, to belive she wanted him to make love to her. She could not remember one, although she was honest enough to admit that at one time she had been very physically aware of him.

She tried not to think about the incident. It was best put right out of her mind — and Jeff's. If they were to continue living at such close quarters on this island, then they must at least try to keep up appearances of being on reasonably good terms. Otherwise Suzanne would feel the tension and worry on her behalf and it would spoil everyone's holiday. She longed to tell Suzanne everything but could see at once that to do so was selfish. It would take the load off her own mind and lower it on to Suzanne's. Jeff would know better from now on. She'd made it more than clear that she disliked him. He'd have to keep his distance and leave her alone now.

Gently, the thought of Greg stole into her mind. He'd been so kind and thoughtful. Greg was really to be trusted — she knew she had not the slightest need to be afraid of him. And he liked her — he'd admitted he'd been jealous of Jeff and that he thought she was pretty and fun to be with. She was lucky — more than lucky to have Greg for a friend.

When Maria came in with her supper, Phil's eyes were closed and there was a look of intense happiness on her face as she slept.

★ ★ ★

Jeff tapped the butt of his tiny gun on the palm of his other hand. The man opposite him watched him apprehensively. It was clear that Jeff was getting very impatient and the man was afraid.

In perfect French, Jeff said:

'You'd better not fool with me, *mon vieux*. If I find you lied when you said the rendezvous was Tuesday, I'll kill you. And don't think that's an idle threat. I have only to say I shot you in self-defence. All this . . . ' Jeff's arm swung round, pointing to the boxes stacked against the cave walls ' . . . this will go heavily against you. I'd have every right to shoot a drug dealer.'

The olive skin of the French Moroccan turned even more sallow. He did not doubt that the American would carry out his threat. His head still throbbed from a blow from the butt of Jeff's gun, delivered on a previous meeting a few nights ago.

The man shivered. He'd come up against some thugs in his time but never a youngster like this one — cold, ruthless and vicious.

'Monsieur, I promise — I swear to you — the rendezvous is Tuesday — always before it is Tuesday. I cannot understand — unless my contact saw the motor boat leave the island and does not think it safe to come tonight. Unless he is quite certain he can anchor off the island unseen, then he will not come.'

Jeff tried to control his anger. It seemed as if this was not his lucky day — first the frustration of failing to make any headway with Phillida — and now this. The fact that he would have to wait another day for the hush money he'd been promised, mattered not in the least. What drove him mad was the feeling of anti-climax. He'd waited over a week for this moment and his nerves were strung tight with excitement. To have to go back to a dull uneventful evening at the villa without having achieved anything was as irritating as the thought that he was not in control of the operation.

He swore softly. The Frenchman cowered back against the damp wall of the cave, his ugly little face twisted with apprehension. Jeff studied him scornfully. He had always despised anyone who feared him. When he'd come upon the fellow the first time, sleeping, and had kicked him into wakefulness, the man had cried for mercy before he knew even what Jeff wanted. It had been child's play to Jeff, getting him to agree to a cut of the spoils in return for his own silence.

The set-up was too simple to have much appeal to Jeff. Once a month, Alfonse's 'contact' anchored off the island in his yacht and rowed ashore in a dinghy. The half-dozen boxes of contraband were loaded on board and Alfonse was paid his cut. Alfonse was then rowed back to the island together with sufficient stores to last him the next four weeks. Some time during that period, another yacht called and left more boxes in the cave to be collected by the first man. Alfonse had spilt the beans after little more than a bit of arm twisting by Jeff. It was obvious that he was only a kind of glorified caretaker and that the other two men were the Big Boys. They were the ones that interested Jeff. He'd waited for this moment to meet Big Brother Number One and arrange a much bigger cut in return for keeping quiet about their activities.

A pity, thought Jeff, that the boxes did not all contain drugs. That would mean really big money. But Alfonse seemed scared even of the word and told him that most of the goods were things like costume jewellery and watches being smuggled out of Europe via Tangier to England. The stop at the island was essential for it gave the man taking the stuff out of Tangier four weeks in which to pick a suitable occasion for loading up and getting away. He was not dependent upon a rendezvous in mid-ocean to hand over the goods. The second man called at the island on the first Tuesday of each month to pick up what was waiting for him and could take his time getting it into the British Isles. No one was pressed for time and this made the whole show a lot less dangerous.

In view of the fact that the proceeds had to be split three ways — and even if Alfonse's cut was a good deal smaller than the Big Boys', Jeff could not see anything really big going into their pockets. But drugs — they fetched better money. There was a small consignment going this time, Alfonse informed him.

Jeff meant to discuss the situation with the man he called Big Brother Number One. If it couldn't be better organised, then he intended to think up something else. He was sick to death of having to accept handouts from his so-called stepfather. Not that the man was ungenerous but on a matter of principle, so he had informed Jeff, he thought it was wrong to let a young man have too much ready money.

Too much! Jeff told himself furiously.

How could you have too much if what you wanted in this life was to be totally independent; to be able to buy what you wanted without having to ask anyone for what was your natural due. It never seemed to cross Charles Kingley's mind that it was Jeff's own money he handed out so 'generously' at the end of the month. After all these weeks, he was bored to tears with the Kingley family's domestic bliss. He wanted to be free of them — to get to Europe and really live it up. The only distraction was the girl and she'd proved a dead loss. Silly immature little thing — he despised her — yet it did not stop him continuing to desire her. He'd have her in the end — just as he'd have everything else he wanted. There had to be a way. There always was a way if you stuck to a problem long enough and were prepared to go to any lengths to achieve what you wanted.

He glanced at his watch again and his mouth tightened.

'I'll be missed up at the house if I

wait much longer. You said seven o'clock — it's nearly eight. Can he still come?'

The man shrugged his shoulders in a typically French gesture. Jeff hit him hard across the face and Alfonse gasped with pain.

'Answer me!'

'Monsieur, I don't know — how can I say? Other times, he is always here before this. Please, monsieur, do not hit me again. I do not know if he will come now.'

Jeff resisted the desire to hit his informant a second time. He said:

'I'm going back up to the villa for dinner. If your contact arrives while I'm gone, you're to make him understand he's to wait here till I come.'

'But, monsieur, suppose he will not wait? Suppose he thinks it is a trap and that you will return with the police?'

'Police — on this island. Don't be a damned fool. Make him wait, O.K.?'

'Monsieur, I cannot make him do what he does not wish. I am only his employee — he will not take orders from me.'

'Then that's your problem!' Jeff said cruelly. 'If I come back and find the stuff has gone, I'll shoot you, Alfonse. Get that into your scrawny little head. And if you do the disappearing act, that'll go badly for you too, because I shall give your description to be circulated to every policeman in Europe — they'll catch you sooner or later.'

'But, monsieur, I . . . '

Jeff left him still protesting in his high whining voice. He went back to the villa by the secret passage, taking care to lock the heavy wooden door behind the stone panel in the wall of the cellar. When he'd first found the door, there had been no key — but Jeff had stolen a heavy padlock from the gardener's tool shed and had fixed it up so that he could lock the door from the inside. Originally the precaution had been to stop anyone who accidentally found the door behind the cellar wall and so discover the passage, too, but now it

181

had another purpose — to keep Alfonse and his friends out. It might be necessary — just in case Alfonse's boss took it into his head to bump Jeff off rather than split his money yet again. Jeff was not the one to take any chances.

The cellar led up to the kitchen but for obvious reasons Jeff did not go back into the villa this way. He eased his body through a high, narrow window which opened on to soft ground, then put his arm back through the window and carefully scooped up a handful of gritty dust. This he scattered with slow concentration over the marks left by his body. It was quite impossible when he had finished, to see that anyone had been in or out of the cellar by that way.

10

Darling Gran,

Thank you a thousand times for the beautiful wrap. It is perfectly knitted and I am so pleased with my lovely birthday present. It will be wonderful for putting round my shoulders when the evenings are cool.

I had a marvellous birthday — Charles took us all over to the mainland for the day and paid for us to go water-skiing. Greg was very good but Murray and I were pretty hopeless though we had loads of fun trying. It's a fabulous sport and we're all going again next week.

You asked about the children — they are as brown as berries and both tremendously well. Little Rupert is walking — toddling, really, and we all have to keep an eye on him as he is very adventurous now he has found his feet! Most afternoons, after his nap, we put him in his playpen by the swimming pool and he watches us in the water. He swims, too, of course, riding on Charles' back which he loves. Jenny swims like a fish and has dispensed with her arm-bands for good and all. Murray is teaching her to dive.

The weather is much hotter than when we arrived. It was a good idea coming so early in the year as now we are all acclimatised and are beyond getting sunburnt. I feel so sorry for Charles who has to go back to England next week. I read in the paper that it was 'dull and cloudy' in London — it doesn't bear thinking about and I do hope, Granny, that you are at least catching occasional glimpses of the sun. I wish I could put some in a bottle and send it to you.

No, I'm never bored. We play games in the evening — Greg has taught me chess; and the whole family play Monopoly and Scrabble and sometimes we put on records and dance. As I'm the only girl, I'm never short of partners.

You asked about my birthday presents. Well, Suzanne and Charles gave me money in case I see any clothes or anything I'd like to buy on the mainland or to save, if I prefer. I expect I'll do the same as I do with my pay — spend half and save half! Greg gave me some gorgeous French perfume, Murray some chocolates. Jenny gave me a picture she had coloured herself and a box of handkerchiefs. Rupert gave me just a nice big kiss!

About Jeff — yes, he's still here. If I haven't mentioned him recently, it's because we aren't getting along very well. He's terribly jealous because he knows I prefer Greg. Then there was the birthday present episode — Jeff tried to give me a bracelet. I didn't want to hurt his feelings by refusing but I didn't want him to think I was willing to accept expensive presents from him. Jeff kept saying it was a cheap bit of paste but I showed it to Suzanne and she said it was real diamonds and must have cost Jeff a fortune. Of course, I returned it to Jeff at once and he was furious. Then Charles asked him where he had got so much money and he said it happened to be a piece of jewellery that had belonged to his mother and he could give it to whom he pleased.

It was all very awkward for me. Suzanne and Charles know I don't want to get involved with Jeff in any way and yet they could hardly reprimand him for giving away his own possessions. Since then, Jeff hasn't spoken much to any of us and whenever Charles will let him, he takes the motor boat over to the mainland. I don't know what he does over there but Greg says he came back a bit tight the other night and tried to pick a fight. Greg ignored him because he felt Suzanne wouldn't want a brawl in her house where he was a guest and Jeff called him a coward and then Greg did go for him and Murray had to break it up. Next morning — that was yesterday, Charles read the riot act to Jeff and he turned and said it was all my fault — that I'd been playing him off against Greg. I was terribly upset and went straight to Suzanne and asked her to accept my notice but she wouldn't hear of it and blamed Jeff, whom she doesn't like. It all blew over with Jeff apologising, somewhat surprisingly, and on the face of it, everyone is friendly again, but I'm sure it is only on the surface.

I've tried not to talk too much about Greg, because I don't want to bore you but I can't help it, Granny, it gives me pleasure just to write his name. He is so nice — I KNOW you will like him tremendously when you meet him. I know it's awfully soon to get serious but the fact is, I am seriously fond of him — even a little in love with him and although he hasn't actually said so, I know he feels the same way about me. I keep telling myself that I'm just flattered and pleased because I finally have a real boyfriend — the first I've ever had! — and that what I feel for Greg probably isn't real love at all. But I'm sure in my heart that I'll never meet a boy I like better. Murray told me he had never known Greg stay interested in a girl for so long a time. Of course, Greg has had lots of girlfriends but I don't mind. He's so attractive I'm not surprised and if he likes me best, that's all that is important. Don't be afraid that I am taking the whole thing too seriously — Suzanne warns me every day about doing so; and really I'm not. I'm just happy and we laugh and have fun and sometimes Greg kisses me and that's all there is to it . . . .

Phil's pen poised over the writing-pad. That last sentence was a half-truth. It was true that Greg kissed her sometimes but she had omitted to say how deeply his kisses affected her. Perhaps Greg himself did not know. His kisses were gentle and between them he would smile and tease her a little and then kiss her again. Perhaps he never saw beyond that brief contact of their lips to the vague longings he evoked in her body as it awakened slowly but surely to love. There were moments — usually at times when Greg was briefly but fiercely passionate — when she would find herself thinking deeply about moral issues. There'd been many times when she'd heard such subjects discussed by her classmates at school — many of whom no longer considered it such a good idea to give themselves wholly to the boy they loved before marriage. Phillida had never taken part in such talks for she had never felt the slightest desire to make love in that way to any boy. Now, brought up from her subconscious, memories of the arguments between her school friends flooded her mind. The way she felt for Greg was at times frightening because right or wrong, she knew she wanted Greg to hold her so close that their bodies were as one; she wanted to make him happy; to give him joy, pleasure, anything that would please and content him. She wanted him to touch her — not just to hold her hand but to caress every part of her. She knew it would be wrong to go all the way and yet she could not *feel* it to be wrong.

How Greg felt, she was by no means sure. Once when she had responded to him particularly passionately, he had quickly drawn away from her, saying:

'Not with you, Phil! Not with you, darling! I want you too much to trust myself.'

Phil thought often about that word 'trust'. She trusted him implicitly and yet she doubted now if *she* could trust *herself*. She wondered if Greg, more experienced than she, guessed this and therefore set out to keep their moments alone together as light-hearted as possible. And they were not very often alone, although they could have wandered off together anywhere on the island if they had wished. Somehow it was easier when they were in company. In the presence of Murray, Suzanne or the children, Greg could reach out quite naturally to hold her hand; could lie in the sun with his head propped up against her waist; pay her teasing compliments. Alone they were both much more constrained. Phil wished Greg would talk about their relationship but he always avoided doing so. It made her uneasy. His reason for keeping their affair very light and casual *could* be that this was the way he wanted it; that he was not nearly so deeply emotionally involved as herself.

Only Suzanne knew how she felt. Suzanne was like a wonderful elder sister to her and not in the least like an employer. She seemed to be able to guess just what Phil was thinking and feeling. Only last night she had sat on the edge of Phil's bed and said gently:

'You're very intense, Phil. Perhaps this is because you've led such an uneventful life up to now. Greg is your first love, isn't he?'

She had started to deny that what she felt for Greg was love but Suzanne's raised eyebrows stopped her halfway. They both smiled.

'How can I be sure it *is* love?' Phil said defensively. 'I mean, I've no yardstick.'

The smile was still on Suzanne's face — not derisive but sympathetic.

'Just you keep on doubting it, Phil. I'm so afraid you might get hurt. I think you should keep this friendship with Greg casual — if you can.'

'Because you don't think he feels the same way about me?'

The smile left Suzanne's face.

'I just don't know, Phil. Greg is sweet — I like him very much indeed. And it's obvious that he's very attracted to you. But whether this is the beginning of love — I don't know. I can't forget that his parents called him irresponsible. He may be the kind of boy who falls in and out of love a dozen or more times before he meets the one girl he wants to marry. He's so very young still — and so are you. I worry because I don't think you two are the same type. You are the kind of girl to love once and that will be that. It was the way I fell in love with Charles.

Phil sighed. She was envious of the security Suzanne had; not the financial security but the delight that must come to any woman happily married to the man she loves. Of course, she did not want to get married yet. First there was university — but none the less, she envied Suzanne.

Phil pulled the writing-pad towards her and concentrated on finishing her letter to her grandmother.

I do hope, Granny, that nothing I have written will worry you. There is absolutely no need because Suzanne is like an elder sister to me and I would not do anything of which she would disapprove. I can't get over how wonderfully lucky I am to have this marvellous job with such a very sweet employer.

I must end this now as it's nearly

Jenny's bedtime. It's earlier than usual because I am going over to the mainland with Greg and Murray for an evening's dancing. They have found a very good disco they want to take me to. Greg says it'll be great!

Very much love, Granny darling,
From
Phillida

★   ★   ★

With Rupert tucked up and nearly asleep in his cot, Suzanne turned to her husband and linked her arm in his.

'I wish you weren't going home next week, darling. I'm going to miss you so much.'

He kissed her and patted the hand that rested on his arm.

'I shall miss you, too. I hate to go but I've been very lucky to have had a whole month.'

'You really think you might be able to get a long weekend before we come back?'

'I'll try my hardest — you know that.'

She followed him into their bedroom and sat down at her dressing-table whilst he began to change out of his shorts.

'Charles!'

Something in her voice caused him to look up anxiously.

'Something wrong?'

'Well, not really. I . . . I just want your advice. It's about Phil. I think she's falling in love with Greg.'

Charles relaxed, grinning.

'So what! That seems a very normal thing for her to do.'

'I know! But I'm not sure how he feels about her.'

Charles pulled on a dressing-gown and stood behind his wife, his hands resting lightly on her shoulders. He smiled at her in the mirror.

'Darling, you can't juggle around with other people's love problems. The two of them will have to sort it out for themselves.'

'But, Charles, they're both so young

— especially Phil. And I'm responsible for her whilst she is here with me. I promised her grandmother I'd treat her like my own daughter.'

'Then do that,' Charles said soberly. 'You would trust your own daughter, wouldn't you? Suppose this were Jenny at the same age? Phil knows what is right and wrong.'

Suzanne sighed.

'Yes, but it isn't just that. If Greg is just attracted and nothing more, Phil's going to get hurt. She's completely inexperienced, Charles. Suppose she thinks that letting him make love to her will ensure he falls in love with her. It *could* happen.'

'But it isn't likely!' Charles said comfortingly. 'For one thing, I don't think Greg would suggest such a thing. I know we read a mass of articles and statistics on the immoral behaviour of teenagers, but they aren't *all* like that, darling. Kids aren't so promiscuous these days, and anyway I don't think Greg would dream of trying to seduce your precious Phil.'

Suzanne sighed.

'No, I suppose you're right. All the same, I did wonder if I ought to suggest the boys leave the island. But I don't want them to go myself. I like them both very much indeed, and it was a wonderful idea having them here. Do you know, Murray has nearly taught Jenny to dive? And Greg is so good with Rupert. The children love them and I like having them around. They aren't a bit like . . . '

She broke off, but it was too late. Charles's face darkened.

'Like Jeff? You really do have it in for him, don't you, Suzanne. I can't say I like him all that much myself but I still can't understand why you actively dislike the boy. I don't think you make allowances for him.'

'But I do — or at least, I've tried. I tell myself that he had a difficult childhood, losing both parents and living with an aunt who spoilt him. But none of that makes much difference. I don't *trust* him, Charles.'

'But why? What has he ever done to make you distrust him?' Charles' voice was genuinely puzzled.

'I don't know!' Suzanne shrugged her shoulders helplessly. 'It's his manner — it's ... oh, I can't explain it, Charles. I just *feel* it. Phil does, too.'

'Well, that is more understandable. Jeff's pretty smitten with the girl and she takes no trouble to hide the fact that she prefers Greg. No wonder Jeff is a bit surly and diffident.'

'Charles, you were talking just now about my trusting Greg not to try and seduce Phil. If it were Jeff, I really *would* worry, I think he'd do anything to get her. I've seen the way he watches her — he sort of broods. Oh, I wish you weren't going home.'

Charles moved away uneasily. Suzanne was not the type to panic and he felt perturbed.

'At least you're not still worried about the mysterious intruder?'

Suzanne smiled.

'No, I don't believe that he ever existed. Those 'signs' are probably explainable. No, I'm not frightened of an imaginary man. It's Jeff . . . '

'Darling, don't be silly. He's just a boy. What possible harm can he do? Anyway, this answers your other question . . . don't send the other two boys away. They will look after Phil. And you and the children. I'll have a word with them both before I go — tell them I want them to look after you girls for me. That will appeal to their masculine ego.'

Suzanne said no more. Charles didn't seem to understand that her fears were not physical. It was the intangible threat that seemed to emanate from Jeff which she feared. Maybe Charles was right and she just imagined it. But the boy had been very quiet these last few weeks — surly and uncommunicative. He wouldn't join in with the other three young ones. For instance, he had flatly refused to join them tonight at the disco. It could be he was just sulking because of his jealousy of Greg. But he wasn't taking his defeat very well.

'Forget him!' Charles said easily as he walked through into the adjoining bathroom. 'He's only a kid. If you have any trouble with him, telephone me and I'll send for him to come back to London.'

Suzanne wished fervently but silently that Jeff could be sent back to England now.

11

The two men stood staring at Jeff, their faces reflecting their uneasiness. Alfonse's thin, swarthy countenance looked even more like that of a weasel than usual. The other man — nearly bald with fat oily skin — was chewing his full lower lip. His podgy hands were working as if he were kneading dough.

'Well, Viellard?' Jeff's voice was curt but he was the only one who seemed completely relaxed and at ease.

The fat man, Viellard, screwed up his eyes and gave a quick shake of his head. The heavy jowls trembled as he did so.

'I don't like it! No, I don't like it at all.'

A thin smile flitted across Jeff's face.

'Then that's too bad. You'll just have to get used to it, won't you?'

Alfonse looked at his compatriot nervously. Viellard's expression became for a brief moment authoritative.

'You seem to forget, my friend, that I control this outfit.'

Jeff laughed — scornfully and without humour.

'You mean, you *did* control it. I'm not *asking* you to do what I want, Viellard. I'm *telling* you.'

For a moment, the man remained impassive. Then his face twitched and he said nervously:

'I don't like it. Smuggling has its dangers but this thing you have planned . . . ' He spread his hands palm outwards. 'Kidnapping is a very dangerous game. If anything should go wrong, and the child should die . . . that would be murder.'

'You're not just stupid, you're a coward!' Jeff said quietly. The Frenchman's hand went with surprising speed towards his pocket. Jeff, however, moved faster. A smile spread across his face as he pointed his own gun at his companion before the other had even succeeded in reaching his.

'Slow down, Viellard. If you kill me, that, too, is murder. And murder without any point to it since you gain nothing by my death.'

The Frenchman swore softly but his hand came away from his gun. He said more quietly:

'I still don't like it. The police are bound to search this island metre by metre. They will find the cave. We shall not be able to use it again.'

Jeff shrugged.

'You won't need to use it again. Think, Viellard . . . you will be rich enough never to have to smuggle anything anywhere.'

'How do you know the man, Kingley, will be able to pay?'

'How many more times do I have to explain this to you. I *know* how much money he can put his hands on. It is my mother's money he controls — five hundred thousand pounds.'

'But you said it was in trust . . . '

'With my stepfather as sole trustee. Think, man. Try to imagine that it is your son who is lost. Would you not do anything at all to get him back alive? And I shall be there, encouraging my stepfather to use this money — making his conscience easier. As sole trustee he could if he wants — and no one can stop him. I'm the only person who could argue the toss and I shall be there, offering him a signed paper relinquishing my interests.'

'Won't he think that strange — coming from you?' The man's voice was unintentionally sarcastic.

Jeff's face was amused.

'Perhaps. I don't think he has too good an opinion of me, but you don't know Charles Kingley — he belongs to the old school type you know — every man honest and decent until he's proved to be otherwise. Kingley will want to believe I'm really 'rather decent'. Of course, I shall suggest that he recompense me from his own money in due course. He'll probably offer to do so anyway.'

Viellard began to walk round the

small enclosure of the cave. Alfonse's eyes followed him.

'And you — what do you gain by this? The money comes to you eventually in its entirety. To take it now, this way, you lose half.'

Jeff nodded, his face still amused.

'Charles Kingley could live to a ripe old age. I might have to wait thirty years for that money — *thirty years*, Viellard. I'll be too old to enjoy it then. Half a million *now* will do us very nicely.'

For the first time, Alfonse spoke.

'Twenty-five thousand pounds for me is not worth the risk. I have the same risks as you two and . . . '

'Shut up!' Jeff interrupted brutally. 'You are lucky to get so much. You have only a very small part in the danger.'

'But, monsieur!' The man's voice was a whine. 'It is the worst part. You say I have to be the one to take the child, then I must keep him here until dark. It is the worst part . . . ' His voice had begun to rise with fear.

This time it was Viellard who cut him short.

'*Nom de Dieu*, Alfonse, stop being a fool. This child will not be taken at all until he is absolutely alone. This part of the plot at least I can approve. Our friend here tells me that there is an arrangement for the two English boys and the girl to go water-skiing from the mainland on Friday. Something will be put in the girl's food or drink to give her a very bad headache so that she will remain on the island and *l'Americain* will take her place. This will leave only the two women on the island with the children and the servants. At some time, the baby will certainly be alone. You will conceal yourself in the fir trees and take him only if there is no one about. Therefore you are in no danger.'

'And if he cries?'

Jeff put his hand in his pocket and drew out a small box. He handed it to Alfonse.

'This is something to appeal to you, Alfonse — dope. There are pills here

206

which will put the child into a deep sleep. He can be given two at a time; one will make him drowsy, two will render him unconscious but in no danger. Understand this clearly, *he must not have more than two every four hours*. To give him more is to risk him dying on us and then . . . '

'Supposing he dies anyway?'

'Idiot!' shouted Viellard. 'He is a fat, healthy child. It will not hurt him in the least to be unconscious for a few hours. There is no telephone to the mainland and the motor boat will be away from the island. When the boys return they will be informed the child is missing and monsieur here will at once take charge. He will instruct the two English boys to begin a search of the island whilst he takes the motor boat back to the mainland to report to the police. First, however, he will pick you and the child up. My yacht will be lying off shore and I shall be waiting to take you and the child on board. By the time *l'Americain* reports to the police, you will both be safely on board my yacht. After a suitable interval but *before* the police decide to enlarge their search beyond the island, we shall be on our way to Tangier. There we will remain with the child until the ransom money is paid. It is a good plan. If we are careful nothing can go wrong.'

Jeff frowned.

'Never be too sure of that,' he said thoughtfully. 'It is possible the English boys might argue as to who shall go for the police but I think I shall be able to overrule them on this. The other danger is that someone here on the island might notice that I do not take a direct route to the mainland, but circle the island first. I intend to cover this by saying I want to check that there is no boat hidden in one of the bays that could be used to take the child off the island. This will seem a natural precaution and one they will welcome; if there is no boat to take the child away, then they will be fairly sure he is still here and the police, when they arrive, will concentrate their search here and not on the mainland.'

'There is a certain danger in transferring the child to my yacht!' Viellard broke in. 'However, if we do this with the boat between us and the shore, no one will see exactly what is going on. The child can be put into a reasonably small box; if someone should be watching, it will appear as if I am taking on stores.'

Jeff stood up. He was far taller than either of his companions. He looked down on them and for the first time his inner excitement was betrayed by the glitter of his eyes.

'Then it is agreed? We will make the first attempt on Friday. If there is not a suitable opportunity — and this is for you to decide, Alfonse — then we leave it for another day. This we will decide on the following Tuesday.'

Viellard nodded slowly as if some uncertainty still remained. This was a highly dangerous game — kidnapping. But the rewards were high, too. Quarter of a million pounds! It was a lot of money — the kind of money it would take years to get if he was afraid to take this chance and to continue his petty smuggling.

His face twisted into a grimace. He did not really have any choice in the matter. The American had threatened exposure if he did not co-operate and already he knew the boy well enough to believe him capable of shooting the works and getting away with proving his own innocence. The American had no criminal record and it would be hard to prove he had been involved with them. The boy's word against his own and Alfonse's! What chance would they stand? The alternative was to give up the island and lie low for a few months until they were sure no one was on their trail. But Jeff could give a very detailed description of them and there weren't that many private yachts owned by men of his appearance. No, it was too big a chance to take.

He gave Jeff a malevolent look. No

one had ever dared blackmail him before and that was what Jeff was doing. The price of Jeff's silence was their co-operation in his plan to kidnap the small boy. What was that but blackmail?

'If there is nothing more, I'll be on my way,' Viellard said, his voice surly. But a hand gripped his shoulder and Jeff's voice, lazy and drawling, said in his ear:

'There is one small thing you've forgotten, *mon vieux* — a little matter of ten thousand francs. I think this is what you offered me if the last lot of dope reached its destination safely? Since you are all in one piece, I presume it has done so.'

Viellard's face was a mask of fury. He fought to control himself. 'One day,' he thought, 'this boy will drive me too far.' But this was not the time to quarrel . . . maybe later there would be some way to get even . . .

He pulled out a wallet stuffed with a mixture of French francs, English notes and American dollars. He stripped off a few of each and handed them to Jeff wordlessly. Then he turned and threw some notes to Alfonse.

'Watch yourself!' he said coldly. 'You're the weak link in this chain. You must keep your nerve, understand? Your part will be over very quickly. Once you are on board my yacht, you will be safe.'

'But suppose someone sees me in the motor boat?'

'Don't be a fool!' Jeff said scathingly. 'You will lie flat under the seat. I have already made certain that there is plenty of room for a small man like you. This bay cannot be seen from the villa, the terraces, the wood or the beach. That is the very reason why I have an excuse to come here. I suggest that you stop thinking, my friend, and leave me to make the plans. And if you are capable of intelligent thought, which I doubt, remind yourself that it is not in *our* interest that you should be caught. You would squeal the first moment pressure was put on you. I don't intend to risk that.'

Normally, Viellard would have insisted on opening a bottle of brandy or wine to seal the partnership. But although there was alcohol of several kinds in the cave, he did not suggest they should drink. Something in him disliked Jeff too much to drink with him. He had few scruples when it came to drug deals or defrauding governments of their customs dues; but kidnapping was another matter. It came into a different category, he told himself. This American was bad — ruthless and dangerous. He would not want him as a friend even though circumstances were forcing him to accept him as an accomplice. Not even for a *million* pounds would he have taken on this of his own free will. Only fear that Jeff would get him put away for quite a few years in some dirty French jail had forced him to agree to this plan.

'I'm going back to the house — they'll be noticing my absence!' Jeff said abruptly. 'Until Friday, then.'

He turned on his heel and disappeared up the steep stairs in the direction of the cellar.

The moment he was out of sight, Alfonse jumped to his feet and grabbed the fat man's arms.

'Let's go now, *quickly*!' He was all but crying in his urgency. 'I don't like it — it's too dangerous. Better we should leave this . . .' His arm swept round the cave . . . 'than risk our necks. Monsieur Viellard, I beg you . . .'

'Enough, Alfonse! There is no other way. Not unless we kill him. So long as he is alive, he can inform the police. We should be found eventually.'

'Then kill him!' Alfonse begged. 'Anything is better than this crazy scheme of his.'

'You prefer murder?' Viellard asked coldly. '*Non, merci*, Alfonse. He is not such a fool that he will be lured into some back street in Tangier where he can be quietly knifed. If we kill him here, our confederates in Tangier will realise that it must have been done by you or me, as soon as they read the papers. For the rest of our lives we can be blackmailed!'

'His body could be thrown into the sea!'

'Bodies have a peculiar way of coming in with the tide. Put such thoughts from your mind, Alfonse. I do not say that I would not enjoy killing him but I am not a killer and nor, my friend, are you. We should have everything, our very lives, to lose and nothing whatever to be gained. No, we will fulfil his plan. Afterwards, we shall be free of him, for then *we* shall have something on *him*. The price of our silence over his part in all this will be that he never comes near us again.'

'You think he will pay us our part of the ransom money?'

'He will have to!' Viellard said thoughtfully. 'If he does not, we shall refuse to hand over the child.'

'And if still he will not pay?'

'Then we can threaten him with

exposure. He will not want to take the risk of being involved. If he is caught with all that money on him it would go badly for him. Now, pull yourself together, Alfonse. Much depends on you keeping a cool head. Be very careful at the moment of taking the child. It will be necessary to put your hand over his mouth so that he cannot cry out, but you must take care not to stop his breathing. Whatever happens, the boy is to be kept alive. Remember our lives depend upon it and, if we end up in jail, it's still better than the guillotine.'

They parted quietly, each sunk in their own uneasy thoughts. Alfonse was nervous already and Viellard had thought better than to confess his mistrust of the American. On the face of it, there was a valid reason to mistrust him. There was big money to be had from the stepfather, but at the same time, Jeff wanted the capital now. Why couldn't he wait? However carefully such a plan was made and executed, it carried a big risk and that risk hardly seemed worthwhile for Jeff.

Viellard thought very deeply as he rowed back to his yacht in the darkness. Jeff had not struck him as particularly avaricious. He was of a type who wanted power far more than luxury. Money would give him power, but power over what? Whom? Maybe the boy was just too impatient to wait for his wealth.

A torch flashed briefly a little way to his left. He changed direction and quickened his rowing. Someone called softly to him in the darkness and he called back. Then the rubber dinghy bumped against the side of the yacht and a rough burly-looking sailor pulled him and the dinghy on board.

'Alfonse?' the man asked briefly.

Viellard shook his head.

'Not this time. Get the dinghy in, Maurice.'

The sailor asked no further questions. He'd learned that it was best not to do so if he valued his job. There was good money to be had working for Viellard and that was all that concerned him. He was paid well for his silence. The man could not guess that if things went well, this would probably be his last voyage. Viellard intended to disband his crew and sell the yacht. When he had his share of the ransom money, he would make a completely fresh start — Mexico, perhaps, or Cuba or he might even decide to live permanently in Tangier.

12

'Poor old Phil. How are you feeling now?'

Phil opened her eyes and smiled up at Suzanne.

'Much better!' she said thankfully. She eased herself into a sitting position and added: 'I can't think what was wrong with me. I felt as if someone had hit me on the head with a sledge-hammer.'

'I expect it was sunstroke. You'd better stay in bed for the rest of the day. I can easily manage the children.'

'But, Suzanne, I feel quite all right now, honestly. I'd tell you if I didn't.'

'Well, you ought not to go out in the sun — just in case you had an overdose yesterday. I still think we should have let Greg ask the doctor to come over and see you.'

'I hate doctors!' Phil said. 'And

besides, it isn't necessary. I'm perfectly all right now.'

She swung her legs over the side of the bed and stood up. Just for a moment, she felt a little dizzy but her head soon cleared. She was suffering from nothing worse now than an appalling thirst. She ran her tongue over her dry lips and watching her, Suzanne said:

'I expect you're dying for a cuppa. I'll tell Maria to get tea ready. Tell you what, Phil, we'll have it indoors today, out of the sun.'

As a rule, Maria brought tea on to the terrace overlooking the pool. Rupert's playpen was set up there and it saved moving his various toys and bits and pieces up to the house. Because the afternoon sun was so hot, they were all glad of the shade covering one side of this terrace, shadows thrown by the fir trees which were the outer edge of the wood in which Greg and Murray had set up camp. The comfortable bedchairs and wrought-iron garden table had been laid out there, together with the lilos and plastic cushions.

'I'll go and get Rupert — I left him in his playpen!' Suzanne said. 'Jenny's down there, too. I don't think she has forgiven me yet for not allowing her to go water-skiing with the others. After you'd gone to lie down, she kept on insisting that she was big enough and a good enough swimmer to learn to water-ski and I was a very unkind mother not to allow it!'

Greg had been unwilling to go at all when at lunchtime Phil had suddenly developed that extraordinary headache. Despite the pain, she had been aware of his concern. Then Jeff had surprised everyone by saying he'd like to go in her place. It was the first time for a while that he'd joined in with the others, although he had in fact been much more friendly and pleasant these last few days.

Phil was thinking about Jeff as she washed her face in cold water and changed into a cotton dress. His reversal to his earlier friendliness had seemed to coincide with Charles' departure to England. Yet Phil couldn't see any reason why Jeff should be happier with his stepfather gone. He'd seemed to get on quite well with Charles — better, in fact, than with anyone else.

She sighed and dismissed Jeff as an enigma. At least he left her alone now and only very occasionally did she turn her head to find him staring at her.

She was about to leave her bedroom when she heard Suzanne calling to her. Something in Suzanne's voice caused her to hurry downstairs, shouting back:

'I'm coming, Suzanne. What is it?'

They nearly collided in the front hall. Suzanne's face was chalk-white. She grabbed Phil's arm.

'It's Rupert — he's disappeared!' Her voice, though quiet, had a strong undertone of fear.

'But he can't be far . . . ' Phil began. Then she broke off. 'Not . . . not . . . ?'

'No, he's not in the pool. Thank God

the water is clear enough to see the bottom. That's the first place I looked. I just can't understand it, Phil. His playpen is unmoved — I mean, it isn't tipped up or anything. I don't see *how* he can have got out.'

'Perhaps he toppled over. He can't be far!' Phil said, still not seriously worried. 'Didn't Jenny see where he went?'

They hurried back across the terrace towards the pool. Suzanne said:

'When I came up to see you, to see how you were, I made Jenny come out of the water — I'm always so afraid of accidents. I told her she could pick flowers on the rocks so her back was to the pool most of the time I was away and she didn't see or hear anything.'

'Then at least Rupert isn't hurt,' Phil said comfortingly. 'If he'd fallen or hurt himself, he'd have screamed and Jenny would have been bound to hear.'

Jenny came running to meet them. She looked excited but not unduly worried.

'Have you found him?' she asked. 'I haven't. I expect he's hiding. Naughty Rupert!'

They reached the pool. Despite herself, Phil could not prevent her eyes going to the water. It was as Suzanne had said — clear. She let go her breath.

'Look, Suzanne, if you and Jenny and I each search in a different direction, we're sure to find him. He can't be far off — not at the rate he toddles. I'll go to the wood — Jenny can do the terraces and you the rocks. Give a shout whoever sees him so the others will know he's found.'

She was still quite calm herself, although she could see fear in Suzanne's eyes. She believed what she had said — Rupert couldn't have wandered far away in so short a time. They'd soon find him.

It was cool and dark beneath the trees. Phil walked slowly, looking around and calling softly to the baby. At any moment, she expected to hear his laughter or catch sight of his little red sunsuit bobbing between the trees. But as the minutes went by, her confidence ebbed and she found herself listening for the shouts from Suzanne or Jenny. Surely *they* must have found him since he did not appear to be in the wood.

She came to the clearing where the boys had pitched their tent. A bird flew suddenly from a branch and a twig snapped. Suddenly Phil remembered the 'intruder' and her skin became cold and clammy with fear. Suppose 'he' was still here — *here on the island*. Suppose he had taken Rupert . . .

She pulled her thoughts up sharply. That was ridiculous. Charles would never have left them if he'd really believed there was anyone about. Before he'd left, he and the boys had made a last intensive search of the island but it had been more in the nature of a joke; no one really believed there was an intruder any more. Even Greg, who'd found the footprints and really believed he and Murray had seen someone their first day on the island, had agreed that it was probably just some trespasser like themselves who had cleared off quickly when the Kingley family arrived.

Phil came out on the far side of the wood and realised that she had walked much further than little Rupert could have toddled even with the start he'd had. Suzanne had not left him with Jenny for more than five minutes at the most . . .

She took a different path back through the trees and tried not to hear her own hurried breathing. It was almost a relief to reach the pool once more, to feel the sunlight hot on her head and arms and to see Suzanne hurrying towards her.

'Phil, haven't you found him?'

'Oh, Suzanne, I hoped you . . . '

They looked at one another in dismay. Then they both said together:

'Perhaps Jenny . . . '

But Jenny came skipping up the terrace path calling to them in her clear treble:

'Have you found him, Mummy?'

Suzanne's fingers dug into Phil's arm. She said:

'Oh, God. I'm afraid!'

Suzanne's fear somehow lessened her own. Phil said:

'We mustn't let Jenny see we are worried.'

'No, of course not!' Suzanne let go her arm and drew a quick shuddering breath. When the child came running to her, she managed a fairly normal voice.

'What a mischief Rupert is! We'll just have to go on looking.'

'Jenny, you run up and tell Maria and the other servants that we can't find Rupert. Tell them Mummy would like them all to come and help look for him,' Phil said to the little girl.

Jenny hesitated, looking at Phil questioningly.

'What, *all* of them?' she asked. 'Cook, too?'

'Well, why not?' Phil said, forcing a smile. 'We might as well all have a game of hide and seek. Besides, the more of us looking, the quicker we can find

Rupert and the quicker we can have our tea.'

Jenny's face cleared.

'All right!' she said, and danced off in the direction of the house.

As soon as she was out of ear shot, Suzanne spoke.

'Phil, where can he be? God, I'm so frightened. I just don't understand. I don't see how he could have got out of his playpen, not unless . . . unless . . . '

'I'm sure he just fell out!' Phil said quickly. So Suzanne, too, was remembering the 'intruder'!

'I don't see how he could have. He's so little!'

'Well, perhaps he pushed underneath!' Phil suggested. 'He's quite strong.'

'I shouldn't have left him!' Suzanne said. 'Oh, I wish Charles were here. I wish — Phil, we are going to find him?'

'But of course!' Phil was glad her voice could sound so calm and so certain. She could well understand Suzanne's rising fears but it would not help to give way to them.

Jenny came running back towards them, her face still happy and amused by this new 'game'.

'Look!' she said, pointing to the little procession of servants coming down the terrace in single file — Cook, still in his white chef's coat; Maria, the houseboy, the two Spanish maids and Mario, the head gardener bringing up the rear.

'I told them *all* to come!' Jenny said, dancing up and down on both bare feet. 'Mario was very cross because he was still having his siesta. And Angelique was washing her hair so she was cross, too.'

But when Suzanne explained to them that the baby had somehow vanished a quarter of an hour ago, the kindly Italians and the Spanish girls were at once only too eager to help. They adored children and especially the round, chubby Rupert with his beautiful golden curls and laughing blue eyes.

'He should be easy enough to see!' Suzanne said. 'He has a scarlet sunsuit.'

They all began to talk at once but Mario silenced them. They must look, not talk, he told them, and with much gesticulation, had them fanning out in all directions over the island.

It was Jenny who found the only trace of Rupert — the little cotton sunhat Suzanne had forgotten he had been wearing.

'It was on a bush!' Jenny said, beaming with pleasure because so far she was the only one in 'the game' to have found a clue. 'Wasn't I clever to see it, Mummy? I nearly didn't see it, because the sun was shining right in my eyes . . . '

'Jenny, which bush?' Suzanne's voice was short and sharp.

'Mummy, you're hurting my arm!' Jenny looked reproachfully at her mother who wasn't reacting at all as she had expected.

'Darling, I'm sorry, but this . . . this is terribly important. Which bush, Jenny. Tell me, darling.'

Jenny began to pout. She looked as if

she might cry. Phil, guessing at Suzanne's anguish, knelt swiftly by the little girl and put her arm round her.

'You *were* a clever girl, Jenny. Fancy you being the smallest yet the only one to find something of Rupert's. Why, it might even be you who finds Rupert himself. Shall we go and look near that bush where you found his hat?'

At once, the child's face cleared. This was fun again. She loved playing games with Phil. Right now, she liked Phil better than Mummy who was being rather cross and horrid.

'I'll show you where the bush is,' Jenny said, slipping her hand into Phil's.

Phil gave Suzanne a warning glance. It was essential that she should hide her terrible fears from Jenny or the child might be too frightened to go back. Suzanne bit her lower lip and nodded. Jenny ran off with Phil close behind her and Suzanne followed at a short distance. She could hear Jenny's high-pitched voice; see the little girl skipping along in her normal carefree fashion. She realised that it simply had not occurred to Jenny that her baby brother might have come to any harm. How could such a thought cross her mind when for all her short life, nothing had ever frightened or hurt her? Death, drowning, assault — such words were unknown to her small daughter. Pray to God they were unknown to her baby, too. Dear God, let him be all right. Let him be hiding . . . let him be safe . . .

She began to hope, as Phil did, that Rupert would be somewhere near Jenny's bush. He must have been near to the place. There was no other way in which his sunhat could have got there.

Ahead of her, Jenny paused, pointing. Suzanne saw Phil approach the bush, look beneath it and then around. Suzanne's eyes, too, were searching but there was nothing but an expanse of rock covered with flowering thyme. Rupert's red sunsuit would have been instantly visible had he been anywhere within a radius of two hundred yards.

Slowly, Suzanne and Phil approached one another. Phil said:

'Jenny's absolutely certain this was the bush. I don't see why she should have been mistaken. She had no hesitation in taking me straight to it.'

She looked into Suzanne's eyes and quickly away again. Now she was as frightened as Suzanne. She knew in her heart that something terrible must have happened to Rupert — he could never have come this far, not *alone*.

Suzanne said:

'It's nearly five o'clock. The boys might not be back until seven and we've no way of contacting them — no way at all. Phil, *what are we going to do?*'

She didn't really expect an answer because she knew that there was none. There was no telephone to the mainland; and only the one boat which the boys had used to take them water-skiing. There was absolutely nothing at all to be done.

Phil said:

'We can go on looking. As there is no boat, Rupert must be on the island. We'll find him, Suzanne. He must be somewhere!'

'I want my tea!' Jenny said at their side. 'Why can't we look for Rupert after tea? I'm thirsty!'

Phil put her arm round Jenny's shoulders.

'All right, Jenny. We'll go and find Maria and she can give you your tea. Mummy and I want to look for Rupert a little while longer — after all, he'll be wanting his tea, too, so we really ought to find him as soon as possible.'

'It's a jolly good hide!' Jenny said admiringly as she walked back beside Phil. 'When you find him, can it be my turn to hide next? Please, Phil?'

It was difficult not to speak sharply but Phil realised that the child had no idea how serious all this was. She must caution Maria not to let her know the truth. Jenny had picked up quite a bit of Italian and might well understand Maria's prattle.

Ten minutes later, she was back with Suzanne.

'Mario was on the terrace!' she told her. 'I told him to wait there. It occurred to me we might light a big fire to try and attract attention. If any of the boys happened to look towards the island, they would wonder where the smoke was coming from. What do you think, Suzanne?'

'Bless you, Phil!' the older woman said. 'You're being a marvellous help. I never thought of a fire. It just might work. We can tell the servants to build it high up on the rocks on the inside of the island. You try and round them up, Phil. I'll go and speak to Mario.'

But even as the willing gardener started to collect the necessary wood to begin the bonfire, Suzanne was facing up to the appalling situation they were in. Even if the boys or anyone else saw the fire and came out from the mainland, it would be another hour before they could return for help. Once back on the mainland they could telephone for the police and yet another hour would pass before *they* could arrive. By then it would be nearly dark. By then Rupert would be cold, tired, hungry and crying for his mother, his supper, his cot. If he were alive . . .

But her mind still refused to dwell on such an alternative. Who could want to harm Rupert? Who was there to harm him? He must just be lost . . . lost . . . and it would be dark before there were enough people on the island to make certain of finding him.

Mario's voice spoke softly in Italian beside her.

'Not to weep, Signora. Bambino will be found. I feel it here in my heart.'

The simple words and kindliness of the old man touched her even in the midst of her private agony.

'We must pray to Saint Anthony — the saint who helps us to find that which is lost, Signora!' went on the old man with simple faith. 'And the Virgin Mary, herself a mother, will guard your little one.'

Suddenly Suzanne found herself praying silently and with all her heart. Whilst the prayers could not lessen her fears, at least they afforded some comfort, for surely no God could allow harm to come to a little innocent baby like Rupert. It was only when she stopped that she remembered Charles. He knew nothing of the terror that had overcome her and could do nothing to help her. The only person she needed most beside her in this terrible moment was many hundreds of miles away.

13

It was Jeff who picked up the two French girls, Antoinette and Nicole. They, too, were water-skiing and somehow Jeff managed to get his tow-rope caught up with Antoinette's rope so that they both fell down. Deliberately, Jeff climbed out of the water into the girl's boat, introducing himself and apologising.

The blonde girl was instantly attracted by Jeff ... even more so when he told her he was an American and had two English friends with him.

'I also have a friend with me, Nicole. She is waiting for her turn with the boat.'

'How about you two having a drink with us later on?' Jeff suggested. 'What's your name? I'm sure it can't be pretty enough to do you justice!'

She'd been more than ready to flirt

with him, telling him all her friends called her Toni and he must do the same. Jeff rode back in her boat to the take-off point on the beach and met Nicole, a dark girl not quite as pretty as the blonde but equally willing to be friendly. He hailed Murray and Greg and introduced them.

Greg was uneasy about the suggested rendezvous at the bar of the hotel on the 'plage'. He did not want to spoil Jeff's fun, or Murray's, but he was anxious to get back to the island and see how Phil was getting along. She'd looked rotten at lunchtime and if he only had himself to consider, he wouldn't have come over to the mainland without her. But to refuse to go would have spoilt Murray's afternoon and when Jeff said he'd go along, too, it was too late to back out.

He was conscious of the fact that in a way, he'd pinched Jeff's girl and because of this he ought not to put obstacles in the way of his finding another. Not that Phil had ever been

Jeff's girlfriend but Jeff had certainly hoped she would be until Greg came on the scene.

'What do you think, Murray?' he asked his friend as soon as they managed to get a moment alone together.

'About the girls?' his friend asked, grinning.

Greg gave him a playful shove.

'No, idiot! I mean about getting back to the island as soon as we've finished skiing.'

'Makes no odds to me!' Murray said cheerfully. 'But I can't imagine Jeff being any too pleased if you queer his pitch a second time. He's got his eye on that blonde girl, Toni.'

Greg frowned.

'I know! But I feel we really *ought* to get back.'

'Why?' Murray asked. 'I know Phil wasn't too fit but I should imagine Suzanne can take care of her a lot better than you can.'

Greg smiled but his face soon

became serious again.

'I suppose you'll think I'm the world's prize fool but I have a sort of feeling that Phil wants me.' He shrugged, half laughing at his own suggestion. 'Perhaps I'm just wishful thinking.'

'Well, half an hour or so isn't going to make all that difference,' Murray said reasonably. 'I think we'd better let Jeff have his fun. It'll give him time to make a date with Toni and meet her again after supper. He can bring the boat over by himself.'

The girls turned out to be quite good fun. They were both hairdressers in Paris and had saved all their tips for this holiday in the South of France and meant to enjoy it to the utmost. Jeff was making headway with Toni who listened to everything he had to say with young, eager eyes. Nicole was definitely the quieter of the two. Greg rather liked her. She was shy and reminded him a little of Phil . . .

He gave himself a shake. He was

getting far too serious about Miss Phillida Bethel. If he didn't watch out, he'd be falling in love with her and he certainly had no intention of tying himself down to any girl for years yet. All the same, it was difficult not to fall just a little in love. Phil was so sweet! Sometimes when he held her in his arms, he had the hell of a job to keep himself under control. And with Phil, he just *had* to. She wasn't like the girls he knew at home.

With Phil none of the accepted rules seemed to apply. She was hopelessly, and in some ways, unnervingly innocent. She just had no idea how exciting she was, or how difficult it was for him to be restrained for both their sakes. When she kissed him, it was with her whole heart, as if she were offering herself to him. Yet at the same time, he knew that this was just what he must not take. Once or twice, he'd felt so frustrated that he'd come close to being angry with her. It seemed a deliberate act of unfairness on her part to push all the responsibility on to his shoulders. But he couldn't stay cross with Phil. When she looked up at him questioningly, her eyes enormous and a little hurt, he knew he had no right to be angry. She just did not realise the kind of fire they were playing with when they were in each other's arms.

It worried him sometimes to think what was going to happen to her when she got to university; it would be so painfully easy to rush Phil off her feet so that she didn't know what had hit her until after it was all over. The thought made him feel sick.

Once, he had tentatively broached the subject of morals, asking her views about boy-girl relationships as a kind of springboard, but Phil had said:

'Oh, that! Well, I think each of us has to make up our own mind what we think right or wrong.'

'And have you made up your mind?'

'About what?'

'Well, for instance, whether a boy and

girl should sleep together before marriage.'

'Surely that is up to the boy and the girl concerned? I don't think anyone should sleep around, but I wouldn't condemn a boy and girl who made love to each other if they were very deeply in love and couldn't get married. If they could marry, then there wouldn't be any reason for them to try out sex first, as you put it.'

'But, Phil, it isn't always as simple as that. Suppose they aren't. Actually in love, I mean, but they want each other very badly?'

'Well, I should imagine they'd only want each other that badly if they did love each other.'

He'd given up. You couldn't treat Phil like an ordinary girl. However uncomplicated life might seem to her, she certainly made it very complicated for him at times. The difficulty was that he found it impossible not to become emotionally involved with her. It wasn't just physical attraction — although he was desperately attracted to her; but he *liked* her, too. More than that; he was very fond of her — very deeply fond of her; in fact, he was worried to death he might be very much in love with her.

'You, too, have a girl in England?' Nicole was asking him in her pidgin English.

To his annoyance, Greg found himself colouring. He said:

'As a matter of fact, my girl is out here — over on Topaz Island.' He wondered how Phil would like the sound of that 'my girl'. It made him both proud and worried at the same time. He went on to tell Nicole about the Kingley family and the island.

The time passed swiftly. Glancing at his watch, Greg noticed that it was nearly seven and caught Jeff's eye.

'I think we ought to be getting back,' he suggested.

Jeff shook his head.

'Time for another quick one,' he said casually.

Murray backed Greg up.

'It'll be half past seven before we're back, Jeff, and then we have to clean up before supper. I think we should go now.'

But Jeff laughed off the idea, his arm round Antoinette's shoulders.

'So what if we are a bit late! *You* don't want us to go, do you, *chérie?*'

Both girls pleaded with the two English boys not to break up the party. Greg was torn between his desire to leave and his sense of fair play. Jeff was obviously enjoying himself with the blonde girl . . .

'Why don't you stay on here?' he suggested reasonably. 'Murray and I can go back and explain you have a date. I'll nip back at whatever time you like this evening and pick you up.'

'Do stop fussing!' Jeff said irritably. 'There's absolutely no need to panic — no one is going to worry because we're a bit late for supper. Or are you pining to get back to poor little Phillida?'

His voice was sneering and the taunt

went home. He did want to get back to Phil, but Greg couldn't admit it. He shrugged his shoulders and muttered:

'Well, one more drink then . . . '

Somehow, Jeff managed to prolong the last drink for a further twenty minutes. Even then he would not hurry, dragging out his goodbye to Antoinette by altering the time and place of meeting the next day so often that the girls were left confused and giggling and the whole arrangement had to be gone through a fourth time before finally Jeff was satisfied.

The girls came back to the beach to see them off. As they approached the water's edge, Greg caught Murray's arm and pointed.

'Look!' he gasped. 'The island. Something's on fire!'

There was a moment's silence while they all stared at the faint red glow against the horizon. It was quite dark now — the moon had not yet risen and Mario's bonfire was sending showers of red-gold sparks into the night sky. The flames could be seen easily from where the boys stood.

'Quick!' Greg ordered, wading out to the buoy to unhitch the boat. 'For God's sake, Jeff, get a move on!'

Murray was already starting the motor. Jeff jumped on board. It was impossible to see his expression in the darkness. The girls called goodbye but Greg did not even bother to wave to them. He was already guiding the boat out towards the island, getting as much power out of the engine as he could.

Fifteen minutes later, it was possible to see that the flames were coming from a large bonfire on the rocks. Dark silhouettes of Mario and the other helpers were also visible piling fuel on to the fire.

'It must be a signal to us — something's wrong!' Greg said. 'There's no other reason to light a big fire on the rocks at this time of night!'

He swung the boat round the island and into the bay. At the end of the jetty, someone was waving and calling to them. A moment later, Phil was grabbing hold of Greg's arm.

'Thank God you're here at last . . . Rupert's gone — he's vanished and Suzanne is nearly hysterical with worry. We lit a fire hoping you'd see it and come home. Oh, do hurry! Thank heavens you're here now.'

Jeff caught her arm.

'Let's get this straight, Phil. You say Rupert has gone? Gone where? What exactly do you mean?'

Phil caught her breath. She must keep calm — she had managed to do so until the sound of the boat approaching had somehow brought the full horror of the last few hours home to her. Only then had she given way to panic.

'Suzanne thinks he must have been taken out of his playpen by someone on the island. We — Suzanne and I and all the servants — have been searching since teatime. He just isn't anywhere.'

'He hasn't fallen into the sea or down a cliff or something like that.'

Phil shuddered.

'No! Suzanne and I both feel sure that's impossible. Suzanne only left him for five minutes and in that time he couldn't have got far enough to fall over or into anything. Besides, we found his sunhat on a bush . . . ' She explained that this, also, was further away from the playpen than Rupert could possibly have walked in the time. 'Someone has taken him, Jeff.'

'Then the sooner we get the police out here the better!' Greg said at once. 'I'll go back to the mainland and 'phone.'

'I'll go!' Jeff interrupted. 'But first I think I ought to take the boat round the island — have a quick look at those little bays you can't get to from the top. If someone has taken Rupert, he might be hiding out there where you wouldn't find him easily.'

'No, don't waste time!' Murray interrupted. 'Better get the police out here as quickly as possible.'

'I don't agree it's a waste of time. We want to make sure that if anyone has taken Rupert, they stay here on the island where we are certain to find them eventually. Whoever it is might have a boat and mean to take Rupert off after dark. At least I can make sure that doesn't happen.'

'Yes, he's right!' Phil said. 'Hurry up, Jeff, *please*! I must get back to Suzanne — tell her what is happening.'

Jeff climbed back into the boat and as he restarted the engine, Phil, Greg and Murray began to climb up the terrace path as swiftly as possible. They did not talk, saving their breath for the climb. As they approached the house terrace, Suzanne came running towards them. Her beautiful gold hair was no longer swept up in its usual coronet but was streaming down her shoulders. Her face was streaked with tears. Phil ran to her and put her arms round the trembling shoulders.

'It's all right, Suzanne — the boys are back. Jeff's gone for the police. Don't worry any more — we'll find Rupert soon now.'

Gently, Greg pushed Phil out of the way and put his own strong young arm round Suzanne's shoulders.

'You need a drink, Mrs. Kingley,' he said. 'Come indoors and I'll give you some brandy. You'll feel better then.'

'Oh, Greg, where can he be? My poor little Rupert — it's dark and he'll be so hungry . . .'

'Sssssh!' Greg said gently as he guided her back towards the house. 'You're not to worry any more. It'll all be all right, you'll see!'

For a moment, Phil, too, was calmed by the assurance in Greg's voice; glad that Suzanne had someone else to lean on now.

While Greg was giving Suzanne a brandy, Murray said softly:

'This is a horrible business, Phil. Missing since teatime! With everyone searching, Rupert ought to have been found by now. It looks very much as if there is someone on the island after all.'

'But, Murray, what would they want with a baby? Why take Rupert?'

'Kidnapping?' Murray said, his voice so low that Suzanne could not possibly hear him. 'The Kingleys are very rich — and known to be so around here. They'd pay a big price, wouldn't they, to get their child back!'

'Oh, no, no, *no*!' The full horror of it struck her. She looked up at Murray, her eyes enormous. 'No, not Rupert! Murray, do you think Jeff will have the sense to telephone Charles?'

Greg came across the room to them.

'Mrs. Kingley isn't fit to go on searching. I've told her she must lie down,' he said. 'I'm afraid she's about at the end of her tether. You'd better stay with her, Phil. Murray and I can look, although . . . ' he paused, looking back at Suzanne, stretched out now on the sofa, her arm covering her eyes, ' . . . although I don't somehow think we're going to find him. Anyway, not tonight, in this darkness.'

Phil swallowed. She felt as if something were choking her.

'Then you, too, think he's been

. . . kidnapped?' It was hard even to breathe the word.

Greg took her hand and pressed it tightly in his own.

'Don't you see, Phil, that it is almost better to believe Rupert has been taken away and hidden by someone? The alternative is that some terrible physical harm has come to him. Otherwise, one of you would have heard him cry. If he was anywhere around, say, with his foot caught in a rock, he'd have been howling his head off, wouldn't he? Even if he had fallen asleep somewhere where you wouldn't have noticed him at first, he'd have woken up by now and found himself alone and . . .'

'Greg, don't!'

'I think Greg is right!' Murray said. 'All the same, we might as well go and search with the others until the police come. That can't be for an hour at least.'

Suddenly, Greg remembered his unwillingness to stay on the mainland; his strange anxiety to hurry back to

Phil. Had he had a premonition that something was wrong? If only they hadn't met those girls and stayed on for drinks, they'd have been back hours ago . . .

The same thought must have struck Murray, for he put a hand on Greg's arm and said:

'We'd better get moving, Greg. We've wasted quite enough time as it is. I'll go and fetch the torches!'

Greg looked down at Phil anxiously.

'You're all right?' he asked.

She nodded.

'And the headache?'

'I'd forgotten it!' she said. 'I've been too worried to think of myself. Oh, Greg, what a terrible day this has been . . . it's like living a nightmare and knowing all the time you can't wake up — it's real.'

Greg put an arm round her shoulders and drew her against him. He could feel her trembling through the thin cotton blouse.

'Put on a jersey, darling. You're cold!'

he said, unaware of the endearment. 'And try to keep Suzanne from worrying too much. That goes for you, too. We'll get Rupert back — somehow!'

She wanted desperately to believe this but deep down inside she was afraid; afraid that none of them would ever see little Rupert Kingley again.

14

Viellard looked down at the unconscious child and said:

'He looks terribly pale. You're sure
you didn't give him too much of that
dope?'

Alfonse's face was nearly as white as
the baby's. He bent over the bunk and
put his cheek against the boy's mouth.

'He's breathing. I didn't give him
more than two pills — two at first and
then when he started to come round
about eight o'clock, I gave him another
one. I swear that's all he had. You think
he's going to be all right?'

Viellard looked uneasy.

'Let's hope so!' he said brutally. 'We
don't want a corpse on our hands.'

Alfonse began to shake.

'I need a drink!' he muttered. 'You
don't know what it's been like for me.
Terrible, terrible . . .'

'Cut it out!' Viellard's voice was sharp as he heard the panic in the man's voice. 'Here!' He pushed a bottle of cognac towards him. Alfonse tipped it up and drank greedily. The alcohol steadied him. He sank into a chair and rested his elbows on the table.

'The American took such a long time coming!' he whined. 'And they lit a fire — I was terrified someone would see it on the mainland and bring help before the American got back. You don't know what it was like in that cave with him . . . ' He nodded at the inert little body on the bunk. 'His breathing sounded strange and I thought . . . then there were people searching the island — I heard them calling to each other — the voices sounded terribly near and I was afraid.'

'You would be!' Viellard said scornfully, but he, too, was feeling uneasy. So far, it was true, their plan had gone forward without a hitch. Luck . . . Fate . . . whatever you liked to call it . . . was on their side. The night was pitch black, no moon, and Jeff had been able to transfer Alfonse and the child without it being possible for anyone to see them. Jeff had sworn on his oath that there had been no one watching him when he called in at the cave for his precious contraband! There was no reason for worry, and yet . . . was the American to be trusted?

Viellard searched his mind for some manner in which Jeff could be counter-planning against them. Suppose the man, Kingley, were to offer a reward — Jeff might squeal, but he couldn't do so without revealing his own part in the plot. No, the arrangement seemed foolproof — now Jeff had taken an active part in getting the boy off the island. He was as deep in it as they were.

Viellard got up and went on deck. The fire on the island was dying now. They must have stopped fuelling it. At any moment, the police launches would take off from the mainland. He'd stay and see their lights go past and then he'd give the order to go.

'Sir?'

Viellard swung round and saw Maurice, the largest and the most trustworthy of his crew.

'Yes, Maurice?'

'Pardon, monsieur, but I would like to speak to you.'

'Go ahead!'

The man shifted uneasily from one foot to another.

'Well?' Viellard prompted impatiently.

'Monsieur, it was impossible not to see the cargo we took on board . . . I . . . I don't like it, monsieur!'

Viellard drew in his breath. Here was something he had not taken into account.

'There is nothing to be alarmed about, Maurice. You saw nothing and know nothing.'

'All the same, monsieur, I do not like it!' the man persisted stubbornly.

'Nor, by God, do I!' Viellard thought. Aloud, he said:

'I do not know what you are

thinking, Maurice, but the child we have taken on board is involved in a divorce case. His father, who brought him to us, is removing him from the care of an unfaithful wife. That is all you need to know.'

Did Maurice believe him? He couldn't be sure. The man still stood there, looking down at his feet, his expression surly.

Viellard said:

'The father is American. He is paying very highly to safeguard his child. You, and the rest of the crew, will also have your reward. I heard mention the sum of . . . ' He paused before naming a sum large enough to tempt the fellow without frightening him. 'As we shall be in Tangier in a day or two, that is excellent pay, is it not, Maurice?'

The face became a little less surly.

'If it is just a matter of a divorce, then . . . then I am sorry I troubled you monsieur.' He touched his beret respectfully and ambled away across the deck.

Viellard spat over the side into the water. It was unfortunate the man had seen their 'cargo' as he'd so tactfully called the child. If Kingley were to offer a reward in the newspapers and Maurice saw it, he might be tempted to claim it, especially if his conscience baulked at kidnapping. The fellow was a rascal but no doubt even he had his limits. He'd have to be paid off at Tangier. Perhaps it would be as well to take him into his confidence when they got there — offer him more than he could hope to get from Kingley if he should happen on a newspaper.

Suddenly Viellard's attention was distracted from his thoughts by the sound of approaching engines. He caught sight of the headlights of four boats. So the French police were turning out in force! Time to be on their way . . . the sooner they were out of sight of the pretty island of Topaz the better!

Jeff was enjoying himself. The inspector was in Jeff's boat and was eagerly drinking in Jeff's story about the mystery 'intruder'.

'I cannot understand why you did not inform me of this trespasser weeks ago!' the inspector said thoughtfully.

'Well, my stepfather was quite convinced that if anyone had been there before we arrived — and he half doubted they had — that they must have left very soon afterwards. We searched the island from top to bottom and found nothing — nothing at all. It was very peculiar.'

'And you, Monsieur Aymon? You were not on the island this afternoon?'

Jeff explained about the water-skiing party, and the girls they had met, with whom they had stayed to have drinks.

'And the child was found to be missing at teatime?'

'Apparently!' Jeff replied. 'I really don't know too much about what happened. As soon as I heard he was lost, I came straight back to the mainland to fetch you, Inspector. It seemed the most sensible thing to do.'

The inspector nodded approvingly. The American boy impressed him, not just by his excellent French, but by his coolness. A Frenchman would never have given such a coherent account.

'These two English boys? They are friends of the family?'

Jeff smiled grimly in the dark. Briefly he told the inspector how Greg and Murray came to be staying in the house. He was well aware that he had cast a seed of doubt as to the boys' integrity. After all, *they* had been trespassers!

'All the same, the English boys were with you all afternoon. They cannot have had anything to do with the child's disappearance. And who else is staying on the island?'

'A young girl called Phillida Bethel. She's the children's nurse. Mrs. Kingley engaged her in London before we came out here. She is devoted to the children and Mrs. Kingley. Unfortunately, she was not very well this afternoon and had to go to bed — otherwise she would have been skiing with us.

264

Frankly, Inspector, I don't think there is any murky plot afoot. I think the child just got himself lost. I'm sure he's still somewhere on the island and will turn up.'

'We shall see!' said the inspector. He pulled out a pipe and lit it slowly, instantly reminding Jeff of Inspector Maigret. In the darkness he smiled to himself. For the first time in weeks, life had become exciting again. He swung the boat round into the bay and pulled up neatly alongside the jetty.

'*Nous y sommes, monsieur!*' he said. 'We've arrived!'

Within five minutes Suzanne, the inspector, Phil and the boys were seated in the salon. Suzanne had recovered a little, as if the mere fact that the police had at last arrived had given her new hope. She looked terribly pale but had brushed and combed her hair and re-made up her face. Looking at her, Phil thought inconsequently how beautiful she was. Jenny, thankfully, was fast asleep.

The inspector spoke reasonably good English. Every once in a while, he turned to Jeff for an English translation of the word he wished to use. He questioned each of them, turning from one to another for confirmation of any statement which could be corroborated. When, finally, he stood up, he was smiling.

'Have confidence, madame!' he said to Suzanne. 'Since it is quite certain there was no boat here on the island during the afternoon, it is impossible that anyone could have removed the little boy from the island. This being so, we shall find him — *mais certainement.*' He looked into Suzanne's distraught eyes and added gently: 'It is a very warm night, Madame Kingley. Your son will take no harm even if he has fallen asleep somewhere in the open. I have twenty men with me, all of whom have been trained to search. They will continue until your child is found.'

'Thank you, Inspector!' Suddenly

Suzanne remembered to ask Jeff if he had thought to contact Charles.

'I 'phoned him. He will be coming out on the night flight. He should be here by midday tomorrow. The inspector kindly instructed his sergeant to arrange for a car to meet the 'plane.'

'Thank you, Jeff!' For the first time since she had welcomed him to her home, Suzanne's voice was really warm. 'Now, none of you have eaten, I know. Maria has put a cold supper on the terrace.'

Suzanne herself could not eat. She drank several cups of black coffee but her eyes, like Phil's, were constantly looking towards the flickering lights that bobbed about the island as the police continued their search.

Despite their denials that Rupert could possibly be in the house, the inspector insisted that every room, cupboard and balcony should be minutely searched. As soon as supper was over, this was to be their job.

'I'll do the cellar, shall I?' Jeff

suggested. 'We'll need some bottles of wine up anyway, for the men, won't we, Suzanne?'

Once again she gave him a warm glance of approval. Charles had been right after all — the boy was not really bad. In the present crisis he was behaving magnificently. She felt guilty that she should have misjudged him.

Together with Phil, she searched the bedrooms. They went from room to room in silence, each knowing in their heart that Rupert could *not* be there. He had not yet learned to climb steps.

By the time they all reassembled in the salon, Suzanne was near to tears again. Phil said gently:

'Couldn't you lie down and rest, Suzanne?'

'How could I?' Suzanne replied reproachfully.

'No, I know!' Phil agreed, sighing. Sleep would not be possible until they knew what had happened to Rupert. Greg, Murray and Jeff rejoined the outside searchers. The servants had been told they could retire but none of them did.

The inspector came in again and handed Suzanne a letter. Charles had telephoned and the sergeant had sent out another boat to deliver the message to Suzanne.

'*Coming night flight. Don't worry, darling, Charles.*'

Only then did Suzanne give way to tears again. The inspector nodded to Phil.

'Make her lie down if you can, mademoiselle. If there is anything at all to report, we will bring the news to her. Alas, it is always most difficult for the mother . . . '

Phil forced Suzanne to take some Valium. For a little while, she sat by Suzanne's bed but the inactivity became unbearable. Suzanne seemed to be dozing, so she left the room, and went downstairs to the salon. Jeff was alone in the room, helping himself to some brandy. He glanced up at her as she came in and said:

'I think it's pretty pointless continuing in this darkness. You can't see an inch beyond the torch beam. The inspector agrees with me — they'll go on for another half-hour and then pack up till first light.'

He carried his glass across to the terrace and stood looking out over the island. He was wondering whether Viellard had moved off yet. Probably! He'd want to get out of the way as quickly as he could without arousing any suspicion. He felt a small thrill of satisfaction. Stage one complete. He was in control of a major operation. He knew now what his father must have enjoyed playing his double life during the war — one country against another and himself pulling the strings and raking in the profits from both sides! Power! That was what Jeff had always craved and now at last, possessed. Phillida, standing there so quiet and unsuspecting, didn't know, poor little fool, that he could soon have her, too, if he wanted. He could have anything

— anything at all he wanted.

He said:

'You look pretty desperate, Phil. Maybe things aren't as bad as they seem.'

She looked at him anxiously.

'What do you mean?'

'Well, on the face of it, Rupert ought to have been found by now. One has to admit that it's probable someone else is involved.'

'You really think he has been kidnapped?'

'Well, it looks like it, doesn't it? Remember that case in France not so long ago? Some rich man's son was whisked away from under his nurse's nose in the park. The parents got him back, though, after they'd paid the ransom money.'

'Jeff, don't!'

'Most parents are willing to do anything to get their child back safe and sound. You would, wouldn't you?'

Phil's face was agonised.

'You know I would. I'd give my own

life for Rupert's this very minute if I could. Jeff, do you think the inspector thinks Rupert has been kidnapped?'

Jeff shrugged. He was no longer interested in the conversation. He'd heard what he wanted to hear. Phil did really care about the child — she'd do anything . . .

Phil shivered. It was not the cold but an icy hand that had hold of her heart. Until now she had been able to convince herself that Rupert must be somewhere on the island. Now she no longer believed that he was. Someone, somehow, had spirited him away — and to where? Who knew if they would ever see him again.

Quietly, brokenly, she began to weep.

Jeff stood looking down at her, his face expressionless. He felt no pity for her — nor even, at this minute, any desire. In fact, he preferred her blazing and angry, fighting him. He gave a queer little smile which she did not see. It had suddenly crossed his mind that but for Phil, this fascinating game he was playing might never have come about. At first, the fact that he could milk the smugglers of their profits had seemed enough fun; but that soon palled. His thoughts had turned to something more adventurous, more dangerous. If Phil had been willing to have an affair with him, maybe he wouldn't have had to look elsewhere for stimulus, for amusement. So in a way, Rupert's disappearance was all her fault. How horrified she would be if she knew! Maybe one day, when he felt like it, he'd tell her.

He finished the last of his brandy and put the glass down. Everything was too quiet. He was bored again. He wondered what would happen if he asked everyone to assemble here on the terrace and then announced he knew where Rupert was. He imagined their various reactions and almost smiled. Pity it couldn't be done. He looked once more at Phil and saw her young slim body outlined against the light flooding through the French windows.

Desire, absent a moment ago, swept over him. He drew in his breath.

'Phil!' he said softly. 'Something has just occurred to me — a vague memory I have of a map I once saw of this island when I was a child.'

She was listening to him now, her eyes wide and attentive.

'I think there used to be a secret passage running from the house down to the beach. Suppose it is still there? Maybe whoever took Rupert has hidden him there.'

Phil looked astounded.

'Are you serious, Jeff? You really believe there is a secret passage?'

Jeff grinned.

'I don't know, but we could look, couldn't we? I can't remember much about it but surely it's worth checking on. I wish to God I'd remembered it before!'

Phil's eyes were full of excitement.

'Of course we must look. Let's find the others and . . . '

'Don't be silly, Phil. I don't want

anyone else to know. Think what a prize idiot I'll look if it's all a figment of my imagination.'

'You mean, you aren't sure if you really saw the map?'

Jeff shrugged.

'I saw the map all right, but you know what kids are — I might have imagined the secret passage. It's the kind of thing small boys might dream up. Or it might not have been this island.'

Phil was looking at him doubtfully now. He said lightly:

'Anyway, we could have a look, couldn't we? If there is such a thing, it must be at the bottom of the house — maybe in the cellar. Let's go see!'

Phil hesitated. She had a horror of cellars — and to go down alone with Jeff . . . but she put such thoughts quickly out of her mind. No stone should be left unturned. Rupert had to be found and if Jeff were right and there really was a secret passage . . .

'All right!' she breathed. 'I'll come!'

'But not a word to the others, *promise!*' Jeff said. 'I don't want your boyfriend looking down his nose at me.'

'Greg wouldn't . . . ' Phil began, but Jeff had already taken her arm and was leading her back into the salon and on towards the cellar stairs.

15

It was icy cold in the cellar by comparison with the ninety-degree temperature upstairs. Phil stared around her and shivered, pulling her cardigan more closely around her. Despite the electric light, the room looked gloomy and forbidding, covered as it was with dusty cobwebs and a damp greenish-looking fungus on the stone walls.

'Creepy, isn't it!' Jeff said, hoping to increase her fear.

He had two reasons for bringing Phillida here. Not only did he want to make her suffer for the insult her rejection of him had caused his pride, but he also wished the secret passage to be discovered. It would be a matter only of time before the police found it anyway as their search of the island intensified. But when they did, Jeff wanted to be quite certain that any fingerprints he had left on a previous visit could be attributed to this one — *after* the kidnapping. He made a pretence of searching the cellar and waited for Phil to lose hope of their finding anything. After five minutes, she said:

'This seems pretty pointless, Jeff. I'm sure there's nothing here — no doorway or loose flagstones in the floor — nothing. Let's go back upstairs.'

'Just a minute!' Jeff put a hand to his forehead as if he were thinking deeply. 'Something has just come back to me.' He watched hope dawning on the girl's face as she stared at him expectantly. Then he sighed. 'No, I can't be sure.'

'Jeff, if you've remembered some-thing, tell me, whatever it is. Was it on that map you had?'

She forgot her fear of him and drew closer, putting her hand on his arm and looking up into his face eagerly.

'If I'm mistaken you'll only think I'm a fool and laugh about me afterwards with Greg and Murray.'

Phil blushed.

'That's stupid!' she said nervously, withdrawing her hand from his arm and stepping back a pace. 'Why should I?'

'Because you don't like me very much, do you? You've never forgiven me for that evening on the rocks.'

'Jeff, don't let's talk about all that now. I . . . I'd rather forget it. It was just a misunderstanding.'

Jeff looked down at her, feigning distress.

'You say that but you still believe I tricked you into going with me, so that I could get you alone. From that time on, you've avoided me.'

It was so much the truth that she could not deny it.

Jeff said:

'If I thought you had forgiven me and that we were friends, I could trust you now. As it is, you can hardly blame me for fearing you'll make me look an utter idiot in front of the others if I've been imagining all this.'

'I wouldn't do that. This is far too

279

serious for such petty behaviour. Jeff, *please* tell me what it is you remember.'

'Well, I thought . . . ' He broke off deliberately and shook his head. 'No, it's no good — I just can't talk about it.'

'Jeff, please. This is all so silly — I'll give you my word I won't mention anything you say to the others — my solemn promise.'

'And if I trust you by believing that, will you trust me by sealing our bargain with a kiss?'

Phil gasped. The very last thing she wished ever to happen was for Jeff to touch her. He must know that; must have guessed how she felt about Greg. How could he want to kiss her?

'You see!' Jeff interrupted accusingly. 'You don't want me as a friend and yet you expect me to treat you like one. It's probably all a lot of nonsense anyway. Even if we found the secret passage, there's no reason to suppose poor little Rupert is there.'

The mention of the baby had the effect Jeff desired.

'I'm being selfish — thinking only of myself!' Phil told herself sharply. 'What is one kiss — if it will make Jeff trust me!'

He saw her hands clench at her sides and the slow upward tilt of her face and knew he had won. He stepped forward and drew her into his arms. He felt her body tighten with resistance; felt the shiver of repulsion that went through her. He smiled. Then he bent and kissed her long and fully on the lips. She broke away from him the moment she could, her face scarlet, her eyes flashing.

'That wasn't fair, Jeff. We were sealing a pact of friendship!' She brushed angrily at her mouth with the back of her hand as if to rub away the touch of his lips. Again Jeff smiled. He could take her by force now, if he wished. No one would hear her scream or come to her aid. But to do so would be madness — the moment he let her go, she would denounce him and he would be in serious trouble. No, he could wait. Phil had done what he wanted; shown him by that kiss that she was willing to subjugate her own feelings for the sake of the child. In a little while, he could really bargain with her . . . Rupert's life in exchange for her full co-operation . . .

She was staring at him now, her eyes full of mistrust.

'Jeff, this isn't a trick? You really have remembered something?'

'Don't be a little fool!' Jeff said, the smile gone from his face. 'Of course I have. I remember that the passage came out into a cave on the southernmost tip of the island. If that is so, it must be this wall,' he pointed to the concealed door leading to the cave, 'where the entrance is.'

'But there's a wine rack all across that wall . . . ' Phil began and then broke off, her face full of excitement. 'It could be there's a door behind the rack. Quick, Jeff, help me move it!'

She was already leaning against the iron framework and gave a cry as it moved very slightly.

'Quick, Jeff, help me!'

Jeff watched the ensuing discovery of the door and the secret passage with an amusement he found difficult to conceal. Phil was wild with enthusiasm and had forgotten all about the unwanted kiss. She believed that she was the one to find the passage. When questions were asked later, the inspector would have no cause to suspect *him*.

He suffered a moment of shock when they entered the cave. Alfonse had been stupidly careless. A yellow plastic duck lay in full view on the rocky floor. Phil's quick eyes saw it at once. She picked it up and held it out to Jeff.

'It's Rupert's!' she breathed. 'He must have been here . . . Jeff, we must hurry back and find the inspector. Don't you see, *someone brought Rupert to this cave* . . . '

If Alfonse had been within reach, Jeff would have stuck a knife into him. Now the search would begin beyond the island. It was inevitable that it would do so next day but he had never intended the police should spread their net wider so soon. Damn Alfonse! Viellard wouldn't be many miles distant yet. An air search . . .

He began to argue with Phillida — anything to delay her passing the news to the inspector sooner than need be. But this time she would not listen to him as he tried to convince her that the toy was no proof Rupert had been there. She pushed past him and began to run back towards the cellar door. Jeff dared not try to detain her. Slowly, his temper steadily worsening, he followed her. He'd been a fool showing Phil the cave this evening; that had been a mistake — but a mistake that would not have mattered if that fool, Alfonse, had been a shade more careful.

Within half an hour, the inspector and his men had searched the cave and the little beach, and a sergeant had been dispatched to the mainland with instructions to alert Interpol. The inspector had little doubt now that the child had been removed from the island by boat and that this was a case of kidnapping. All port authorities would have to be notified to search incoming ships. Local police along the entire coast of the South of France must be alerted, too, for a small boat could put in at any isolated bay, land the child and hide until a ransom could be claimed.

For the sake of the child's mother, he hid his own misgivings when he reported back to the villa. A kidnapping taking place in a city enabled the police to set up road blocks and at least stand a fairly good chance of ensuring the child was kept in a certain area. But in this case, the boy could be taken practically anywhere in the world. It was high season now on this coast and there were yachts everywhere. It would need an enormous number of men to search every one.

Suzanne went completely to pieces when she was told that Rupert had almost certainly been removed from the island. While she had still been able to believe that he was somewhere on the island, lost, she could keep on hoping that at any moment, one of the searchers would find him. But now she had to face the fact that it could be days — even weeks, before Rupert was found; that he might *never* be found . . .

When the inspector departed for the mainland, leaving half a dozen men behind as a safety measure, Jeff suggested they should have a conference, without Suzanne, to discuss the situation. Greg, Murray and Phil joined him in the salon where fresh coffee was waiting for them. They were all exhausted but far too worried to think of going to sleep.

Greg drank his coffee black and looked over at Jeff.

'I don't see what *we* can do,' he said thoughtfully. 'It's in the hands of the police now.'

'Yes, but should it be?' Jeff said smoothly. 'If we really want that child back, we've got to let the kidnappers make contact with us *without* the police being around.'

Phil caught Greg's arm, looking up at him excitedly.

'Jeff's right! How can anyone approach Suzanne for ransom money on this island? They'd know the police would be on to them in a flash. There's not even a telephone here.'

'You've got a point there,' Murray agreed.

'I was thinking,' Jeff went on as if the idea had just occurred to him. 'Suppose I go over to the mainland — let the local papers know what's going on and mention that I've booked in at the Plage Hotel. Whoever the men are who have taken Rupert, they will be buying local papers to find out what's going on this end. Then they will know they can contact me at the hotel by 'phone and that I could get word to Suzanne and Charles if it's ransom money they are after.'

Greg nodded.

'Jeff's idea makes sense. In any case,

it can't do any harm. But there's little point in going over tonight, Jeff. First thing in the morning, we'll put the idea to Suzanne. If she agrees, then you can go over directly after breakfast.'

Well satisfied, Jeff retired to bed. Murray stayed for a second cup of coffee before he, too, retired and Greg and Phil were left alone. They sat down on the sofa. Greg took Phil's hand and held it tightly in his own.

'Poor Phil — what a ghastly day it's been. You should go to bed, too.'

'I couldn't sleep!' Phil said wearily.

'Nor could I!' Greg agreed. They sat in silence for a few moments and then he said with a frown:

'I still think it's quite incredible the way you and Jeff unearthed that secret passage. Whatever made you think of moving the wine rack?'

Briefly, Phil explained about the map Jeff remembered seeing as a small boy. Greg listened attentively. When Phil stopped speaking, he said softly:

'So Jeff knew about the secret

passage all along?'

Something in Greg's tone of voice made Phil stare at him.

'Yes, but he didn't actually *know* — he just thought . . . '

'That's his story. But suppose he *had* known all along? Suppose he's in on this whole beastly affair? Suppose he actually planned it?'

For a moment, Phil continued to stare at him wide-eyed, horrified. Then her face cleared and she laughed:

'Greg, that's ridiculous! I don't like Jeff any better than you do but you can't possibly imagine such a thing about him. There isn't any reason, anyway, why he should do such a thing!'

'Isn't there? We don't know how well off Jeff is financially, do we? Suzanne and Charles would be willing to pay anything to get Rupert back. Suppose Jeff needs the money?'

Phil continued to smile.

'You're on the wrong track entirely, Greg!' She explained how Charles had all his first wife's fortune in trust for Jeff. One wet afternoon in London, Suzanne had told her all about it. 'So you see, Jeff would be robbing Peter to pay Paul.'

'And if Charles, as sole trustee, gave Jeff's money to his own son, Rupert?'

'Well, Charles wouldn't!' Phil said at once.

'Yes, I know, but does Jeff realise that? Jeff may be afraid Charles will withhold his inheritance.' Greg persisted.

'No, Greg, that's too far-fetched. And even if you were right and Jeff was involved, the last thing he would do would be to help 'discover' the secret passage.'

Greg sighed.

'I suppose you're right, and I'm barking up the wrong tree. All the same, I can't help feeling that Jeff isn't to be trusted. I've seen the way he looks at you — there's something in his eyes that's bad, wrong . . . oh, I can't explain.'

Phil said softly:

'I can. Jeff's never forgiven me because I made it obvious I preferred you to him. I hurt his pride and he resents it. But that doesn't make him a kidnapper, Greg.'

Greg put his arms round her and smiled down at her.

'No, of course, you're right again. My judgement is probably biased anyway. I've been jealous of Jeff!'

She snuggled up against him.

'You know you have no need to be. I've *never* liked Jeff.'

'Phil!' Greg's voice was suddenly husky with emotion. She looked up at him, her eyes wide and questioning. He swallowed nervously and then said: 'Phil, what I feel for you is much more than just 'liking'. I've been fighting against it for days, but it's just no use. I have to face the fact that I'm falling in love with you. I . . . I didn't mean to tell you.'

'I'm glad you did!' Her voice rang out with a happiness she did not try to conceal. 'I feel the same — exactly the same, but I thought you . . . ' She broke off, suddenly shy.

Very gently, Greg kissed her.

'Of course, we're both a bit young to think of getting engaged or anything like that. But perhaps when we've finished at university . . . if we still feel the same way . . . ?'

'Oh, Greg, yes! Oh, I'm so happy!' Her face and eyes were shining, but a moment later a shadow wiped the smile away. 'How can I say such a thing when poor little Rupert . . . '

'Don't think about it, darling. There isn't a thing we can do. Go to bed now and try to sleep. You'll need all your energy for tomorrow.'

He kissed her again, still gently, knowing that this was not the time for passion.

After she had gone up to bed, he sat on alone thinking about his future. He had no regrets that he'd told Phil he loved her. He could no longer doubt it and somehow he knew that he would not change. He wanted to be able to take Phil home to meet his parents. He knew that they would love her and approve of his choice, even if they were a little surprised that he'd finally made up his mind to settle down to one girl and one only!

The future seemed full of promise. If only this horrible dark cloud were not hanging over them all! If only he and Phil were free to enjoy the last few weeks of their stay on Topaz Island without any horror to make an ugly back-cloth to the scene.

He sighed and suddenly weary, went upstairs to the room he shared with Murray and fell into an exhausted sleep.

16

It was Charles who insisted that everyone but Jeff should remain on the island and, as far as possible, continue to live a normal life. This, he pointed out to his wife, was for Jenny's sake; but to Phil, Greg and Murray, he explained that it was best also for Suzanne. There was absolutely nothing to be gained by moving to the mainland or back to London.

Phil wondered how it was possible for Suzanne to keep up her outward appearance of calm and hopefulness in front of Jenny. The little girl had had to be told the truth for there was no other way of explaining Rupert's absence. They had all, in turn, assured Jenny that Rupert *would* come back although most of them were secretly beginning to doubt it. Five whole days had passed with no news at all of the child or the kidnappers — or at least, as far as they knew. Charles did not pass on to them the information he was given by the inspector.

'I have had investigations made,' the man told Charles on the third day after his arrival back on the island. 'That is to say, the background of each person on this island at the time of the disappearance of your little boy has been gone into very thoroughly.'

Something in the inspector's tone of voice made Charles Kingley look at him intently.

'And you have found out something?'

'Yes, monsieur — something I am afraid you will not be very happy to learn. Naturally, your wife was never under suspicion. The English girl has a clear record and I think we may take it that she could not have had a hand in this terrible affair. This goes for the two English boys also.'

'Then one of the servants?' Charles queried.

The inspector shook his head.

'*Non, monsieur* — not the servants. It is your stepson about whom I have serious misgivings.'

'Jeff? But why? What can he have done?'

'He has a conviction for dangerous driving in the United States . . . '

'Yes, yes, I know about that . . . he told me himself, but the boy was not to blame and . . . '

'He was, in fact, responsible, but it is not this offence alone which makes me uneasy about him, monsieur. Police detectives have visited his aunt, his school and university and some of his acquaintances. What they learned about your stepson encouraged them to go further into his background. You knew that the boy's real father was a wartime collaborator?'

'No, I certainly didn't!' Charles cried. 'My first wife never mentioned it to me. I feel it hard to believe that she would have concealed such a fact from me.'

'Nevertheless, it is a fact, monsieur. He made a fortune out of the war and at one time he owned Topaz Island.'

'That I did know, of course,' Charles broke in. 'My first wife told me when she gave the island to me.'

'So it is more than likely that your stepson knew of the island during his boyhood and that he could have known of the existence of the secret passage. He is the son of his father, Monsieur Kingley, a bad character with a reputation for vicious behaviour which would, I think, horrify you if you knew but the half of it. I have here a dossier on the boy which arrived by 'plane this morning from America. I think you should read it.'

For half an hour Charles was left alone to read what the American detectives had managed to unearth about Jeff's boyhood. As each page revealed yet further and further unpleas- antness, Charles began to feel as horrified as the inspector had foretold. It was clear enough now that the boy he had welcomed under his roof had a rotten if not criminal core.

When at last he put down the folder, Charles felt angry and bitterly ashamed of himself. He should have looked into Jeff's background when he went to the States to bring him home. But he had been so wrapped up in his own selfish desires to get back quickly to Suzanne and the children that he had not acted as any guardian or stepfather should have done. He'd taken the boy at his word and only now did he begin to understand how hopelessly unreliable that word might be. No wonder Suzanne and Phil had instinctively mistrusted the boy! No wonder . . .

He jumped to his feet and called through the door to the inspector who was waiting for him in the adjoining room. A terrible thought had occurred to him.

'Inspector, you don't mean you believe Jeff is actually involved in Rupert's disappearance? Surely even Jeff with his character could not stoop so low as to . . . '

'I'm sorry, monsieur, more especially

as the boy is a relation by marriage, but I am forced to consider the possibility that he is involved. *Look, Monsieur Kingley, at the facts*. Someone took the boy off the island. How was it done? By making use of the secret passage. Who knew about it? Who knew the child's movements? He was taken at a time when no one was in attendance. Everything points to inside help; strangers could not have done this on their own.'

There was a deep furrow of distress on Charles' forehead as the full impact of the inspector's reasoning hit him. That any human being, let alone his own stepson, could be so inhuman as to cause a baby like Rupert to suffer, perhaps even . . .

'You do think we'll get my son back alive?' His voice was tight with his fear.

'I think it is probable. We do not know, of course, that your stepson *is* involved or what his motive can be. In these cases it is nearly always money, although I understand that he is not and isn't likely to be short of this commodity.'

'Most certainly not. I have always given Jeff a very generous allowance.'

'That I can believe, monsieur, but is it possible he wants more? If there is a craving for power? That could mean he wishes to control his own fortune. I understand the money is in trust with you during your lifetime, and that he cannot use this capital?'

Charles nodded. He was too distressed to be able to speak. Jeff might very well be involved — the motive and the means were there.

The inspector looked at his companion with a mixture of sympathy and sternness.

'Yesterday, you told me that your stepson had gone to Nice for a few days. I have been unable to trace how he went. He did not hire a car and he was not seen to leave by train. How then did he go, Monsieur Kingley? Or is it possible that *he did not go* and that you and your family, with the best motives no doubt, have been concealing his movements from me?'

Charles hesitated. His answer might just make the difference between life and death for little Rupert. Jeff's plan to keep apart from the family so that the kidnappers could make contact without fear of police intervention had seemed, when they discussed it, the very safeguard they needed to protect Rupert. Now he could see that this might be a further step in Jeff's own ghastly plans to extort money from him.

The inspector waited patiently. It was not difficult to guess the thoughts going through the father's mind. They would have passed through his own, too . . .

'He's here, in the Hotel de la Plage!' Charles said suddenly, loudly. 'He's hoping the kidnappers will contact him. We all agreed he should do so.'

'Thank you, Monsieur Kingley. Your co-operation makes my job very much easier. I shall, of course, have the telephone and postal service to the hotel watched. It will be done very discreetly — you need not worry on this account. With so many tourists about, it will be easy enough for my men to move about unnoticed. If contact is made, we can take action.'

'But *what* action?' Charles cried. 'If Jeff is involved and you arrest him, his accomplices might panic and Rupert . . . '

'We will not do that, monsieur. We will find out where he is to go to deliver the money and collect the child. We can then have him followed.'

'And the price of my child's life!' Charles said huskily. 'I wonder what they will ask. I had better cable London for a bigger sum than I was able to bring with me. I don't want any delays . . . it has been long enough already.'

But it was another five days before Jeff arrived at the villa, calm, self-assured and smiling.

'They've contacted me!' he announced as the entire family crowded round him, only Charles standing a little apart. Suzanne burst into tears and Phil at once went to comfort her. Greg said eagerly:

'They've got Rupert? He's alive?'

'And kicking!' Jeff said. He turned to Charles and said carefully: 'They are asking a lot of money — a quarter of a million pounds.'

There was a moment of stunned silence. Then Suzanne grasped her husband's arms and with the tears still streaming down her cheeks cried:

'You'll pay it, won't you, Charles? Anything . . . anything . . . '

At once he put his arm round her.

'Of course! What other demands, Jeff?'

'They want someone to go with me. They say that as the child is only a baby, he cannot be set free at a street corner and that it is too dangerous to hand the child over when the ransom money is paid. I've been thinking about it on the way over to the island. Maybe it would be best if Phil comes with me. Rupert knows her and . . . '

'Then *you* are going to hand over the money?' Charles asked quietly.

For a split second, Jeff looked taken aback. Almost at once, he recovered himself and said suavely:

'Well, they suggested it. They think the police may be watching your movements.'

'I see. And where is this meeting to be?'

'Tangier!'

'Tangier!' Suzanne gasped. 'So far away?'

'The distance isn't important!' Charles said evenly. 'All that matters is that Rupert is safe!'

'Then you agree Phil should come with me?'

'Of course I'll go, *of course*!' Phil cried, but Charles remained silent. Had he the right to risk Phil's own safety in this desperate game? She was still a minor . . . in his care.

'No, I think it would be better if one of the boys went!' he said slowly. 'Greg, perhaps?'

Before Greg could reply, Jeff broke in:

'Don't you think we ought to stick to their arrangements?' he said. 'They said 'a woman'. If a man goes, they might suspect something.'

'I'll have to think about it,' Charles said slowly. He felt suddenly afraid. What reason had Jeff to insist so adamantly that Phil go with him? Had he some private motive? If so, he had less right than ever to involve her.

'Please, Mr. Kingley, let me go. Jeff's right — they won't need to fear me.'

'I don't think she ought to go!' This time from Greg.

'But surely she won't be in any danger?' Suzanne argued. 'Jeff can take care of her. Charles . . .'

It was impossible not to see the naked fear in her eyes nor to underrate her anguish, but she did not know what had passed between himself and the inspector.

'I'm going to find the money!' he said abruptly. 'I'll let you know what I've decided in a minute or two!'

He wished desperately that there was a telephone service to the mainland. Had there been, he could have asked the inspector's advice. Now he was in torment — to risk a young girl's life to save his son's — it could be all that. But *was* there a risk? The inspector would have heard about the telephone conversation — be making arrangements now to follow Jeff wherever he went. His men would take care of Phil. She would not really be in any danger.

Alone, he covered his face with his hands and prayed as he had not done in years. He needed guidance, a wisdom greater than his own to make this decision. And then, suddenly, there was an answer to his prayer. Maria knocked on the door and called to him that the inspector was in the little salon asking to see him.

He hurried downstairs and found the family gathered round the inspector. The room was silent. He looked at the

Frenchman and caught a warning glance.

'Ah, good day to you, Monsieur Kingley. I am sorry to disturb you but one of my men reported seeing a boat approaching the island. We hoped that perhaps this was news of some kind but your stepson tells me it was only he returning from his visit to Nice.'

Taking his cue, Charles said:

'Yes, that's right.'

'Then my hopes have been for nothing!' said the inspector with a good imitation of regret. 'In which case, I must apologise again for disturbing you. I would like to say that my men are doing everything — following every clue. We think perhaps there is a likelihood of the kidnappers being in Marseilles. We are concentrating our search there.'

'I see! You'll let us know, of course, if there is anything new?'

'But certainly, at once, monsieur. Now I must be on my way.'

'I'll come down to the jetty with you!'

Charles said casually. 'And by the way, Inspector, if you see our boat going to the mainland after tea, do not concern yourself as it will only be Jeff taking Miss Bethel there for the evening.'

'Thank you for advising me.' He bowed politely to the still silent members of the family and went down towards the terrace path with Charles. As soon as they were out of earshot, he said:

'All is in order. There's no doubt now that your stepson is involved. He spoke to the man from Tangier with complete familiarity. You must arrange for him to fly from Nice — it is sensible that he takes the route via Madrid. He can then be picked up easily by our men in Tangier. I will also arrange for one of my men in plain clothes to accompany him. With luck, monsieur, we should soon have your son safe.'

'And the girl?' Charles asked. 'You think it safe for her to go?'

The inspector frowned.

'There was no mention of a girl on the telephone.'

Quickly, Charles explained Jeff's request that Phil should go with him.

The inspector frowned again.

'This is entirely his idea!' he said. 'But why? I do not understand!'

'I think I do!' Charles said gravely. 'I think he has never got over his desire to impress Phillida. I don't know enough about it to be sure but my wife told me she thought Jeff was in love with her — or at least if it wasn't love, there was something between them. Then Phillida met Greg and Jeff was pretty jealous for a while. We thought he'd got over it but perhaps all the time he has been hiding his real feelings.'

'That explains quite a lot. In which case, we must pay most careful attention to Mademoiselle Bethel. She could be in a different kind of danger.'

'You think I should let her go?'

'Indeed, yes, monsieur. To thwart him is to arouse his suspicion. I give you my word she will never be alone with him. But you must, of course, warn her. If they go to an hotel, she must always at all times lock her door. I do not want to reveal the presence of my men in order to protect her. It is most probable that he plans to seduce or assault her but if she is careful she can evade such attempts, perhaps even allowing him to think she will comply with his every wish once she has the child safely. By that time, he will be in our hands.'

'And she will be in no danger?'

'There is obviously a risk but we shall be there to protect her. It is imperative that we do not allow your stepson to become suspicious. To refuse to permit her to go with him is to show a lack of trust, or that we suspect him.'

Charles returned to the villa with his mind made up but with his heart still gravely concerned for Phillida. There was also the question, would she be prepared to go with Jeff when she knew what kind of person he was?

Jeff, Greg and Murray were standing

on the top terrace talking in low voices. As Charles approached, Jeff broke off what he was saying and asked:

'What was that old fool gossiping about?'

Charles stifled the reproach he'd been about to make. Better to let Jeff imagine he had the centre of the stage.

'Oh, he was on about these men in Marseilles. Someone reported they'd seen a suspicious-looking trio with a baby. There can't be anything in it — not now we know the real culprits are in Tangier.'

'You didn't tell him anything — about the call I received?'

Charles was no actor but he put up a convincing act when he said:

'What do you take me for? I'm hardly likely to do anything to ruin our chances of getting Rupert back.'

'And Phil?' Jeff persisted. 'It's okay for her to come with me?'

'If she's willing!' Charles replied. 'I'm going to talk to her privately.'

'She already said . . . ' Jeff began, but

this time Charles was unable to restrain his temper.

'I've said I intend to talk to her myself,' he said roughly, and walked away.

Greg followed him into the villa. His young face looked grey beneath the suntan. He said in a low, strained voice:

'I know I've no right to be saying this, sir, but I'd be awfully glad if you'd let me go in Phil's place. I . . . I don't think she's safe with Jeff.'

Charles glanced at him sharply. The boy held his gaze with steady blue eyes. He wondered if he dared tell Greg the truth but decided against it. The more the boy knew, the more cause he would have to worry.

'I understand how you feel, Greg,' he said simply. 'But a baby's life is at stake. Some risks have to be taken. And I don't think Phil would thank you for preventing her going.'

'Sir, I . . . I . . . '

He looked so utterly miserable, Charles relented and put a hand on the boy's arm.

'Trust me, won't you?' he said gently. 'I'm well aware of all the possible dangers — *all*!' He stressed the last word. 'Believe me, I wouldn't let Phil go if I were not quite sure in my own mind that, no matter how it looks to you, the risks are negligible.'

Greg bit his lip. There was something in the older man's tone that calmed him and gave him food for thought. He trusted Mr. Kingley implicitly, just as he mistrusted Jeff. Mr. Kingley must have weighed up the position. The inspector . . . perhaps his visit was not quite so coincidental as it had seemed.

'Very well, sir. When will they be leaving?'

'There's a plane for Madrid leaving Nice at 2.40 p.m. If they catch that, there's a connection at Madrid for Tangier that will get them there the same evening.'

It was only then that Greg knew for sure the inspector was in on the whole thing. How else could Charles know the times of planes and connections to Tangier?

'Don't you think, sir, that it might be best if you don't know what time the 'planes depart?' he asked with a smile.

Charles looked at him sharply and for the first time that day his face broke into a smile.

'Good boy!' he said warmly. 'I hadn't thought of that. Nor, it seems, had the inspector. I'm glad you're part of our team.'

'So am I!' said Greg. 'And now I'll go back and tell Jeff you think he's perfectly capable of handling this on his own. Tell Phil I . . . just tell her to take care of herself, for me.'

17

Jeff looked at his companion with a frown of annoyance.

'You're very quiet!' he said. 'You've hardly said a word in the last two hours.'

Phil tried to answer casually.

'It's hot! Besides, I'm worried about Rupert.'

'Well, stop worrying!' Jeff said. 'By tonight, you'll probably have him safely back in your arms, thanks to me. If we'd left it to that fool of an inspector, I doubt if we'd have seen the child alive again.'

With an effort, Phil tried to make her expression admiring.

'Yes, it was a good idea of yours going to that hotel.'

Jeff looked pleased. So far, his plan was working out to the detail. Viellard was a fool to have sounded so terrified on the 'phone. There was nothing to be afraid of. The inspector had his troops marshalled in Marseilles — couldn't be better. And *he* had the money safely tucked into a briefcase — every last pound he'd hoped to get. Charles had paid up without a murmur though God knows how he'd raised so vast a sum in cash in so short a time. Borrowed, probably. One thing was sure, Charles wouldn't get it back. And another thing was sure, *he* wasn't going to give Viellard such a big cut as he'd promised. Viellard had done next to nothing. It was he, Jeff, who'd made all the plans and taken all the risks. Viellard was in such a state, he'd probably accept anything to be rid of the child and any further responsibility.

Phil tried not to see the ugly look on Jeff's face. Ever since Charles had told her the whole terrible truth, she had been unable to think of anything else but that Jeff was evil enough to stoop to risking the life of a little baby like Rupert; to cause someone he knew and who'd been immensely kind to him like Suzanne, such terrible fear and anxiety. Yet even now Phil found it difficult to believe that the young good-looking boy sitting opposite her could be capable of such things. Charles had said:

'He wants something from you, too, Phil. Never be alone with him, *never*. No harm can actually befall you because there will always be an invisible man within a few yards of you; but should you shout for help, it will undo all our hopes for getting Rupert back as it would force the man to reveal himself. You'll have to be very, very careful.'

She hadn't felt frightened then, but now, watching the cruel avaricious expression on Jeff's face, she knew fear. She was afraid it would show in her eyes and she tried desperately to think of something else. Greg! How kindly Charles had spoken of Greg — as if he knew she and Greg were in love and understood Greg's anxiety for her. It must have required almost as much courage for Greg to stay behind and do nothing as for her to come with Jeff.

'Penny for them, my pretty Phillida!'

She blushed and heard Jeff's low laugh.

'What a schoolgirl she is!' he taunted. 'Aren't you ever going to grow up, Phil? Time you did, you know. Have you never been away with a man alone before?'

'Don't be silly, Jeff. We aren't going away alone — not in the way you mean!'

'And what way is that?' Jeff teased. 'As lovers?'

'How can you talk like that when Rupert . . . '

'Can't you forget that brat for one instant?' Jeff broke in roughly.

'No, I can't!' Phil flashed back. 'I can't think of anything but how ill or miserable he might be.'

'*If* he's alive!' Jeff said brutally. 'We don't know if he is!'

'But you said . . . '

'I was only repeating what I was told.

We don't know it's true though, do we?'

She looked him aghast. Somehow this possibility had never occurred either to her or to Charles. Suppose Jeff had not in fact had that telephone call from Tangier? Suppose he'd made it all up, had taken the money and was making his getaway? Then, with immense relief, she remembered that the inspector had overheard the conversation. The 'phone call at least was fact.

'*You* think he's alive?' Jeff asked, watching her face.

'I don't know. I hope so. I've prayed.'

'And you really believe there is a God who answers prayers?' Jeff's voice was scornful.

'I know it!' Phil said simply.

'Rubbish!' Jeff said. 'You live in a dream world, Phil. When it comes down to rock bottom, there's only one person in the whole world you can have faith in, and that's yourself. You can trust yourself, believe in yourself. No one else.'

'And if you fail yourself.'

'I don't intend to do that. What I want, I'll get.' His voice was cool, matter of fact. Phil felt a shiver go down her spine. It was becoming increasingly certain to her that Jeff was not normal — there was something twisted in his mind.

'What are you thinking about now?' Jeff asked, feeling her gaze on him.

'You — what an extraordinary person you are!'

Jeff seemed pleased.

'I guess I don't rate as ordinary,' he said. 'But I didn't realise you'd given me that much thought, Phil. You seemed too taken up with that English schoolboy.'

It was on the tip of Phil's tongue to defend Greg but she bit back her words. Charles had said, *Let him think you'll comply with him, do whatever he wants, until you have Rupert.*

'Beginning to change your mind?' Jeff grinned at her. 'A bit more excitement to be had with me, eh? I could have told you Greg was as dull as ditchwater. But you've taken time coming to your senses; wasted a great deal of time we could have had together — you and me, Phil, and all that sunshine and moonlight.'

He mistook her shiver of revulsion for excitement. He felt no surprise. Everything was going his way right now, so why not Phil, too? After all, why should she have refused him when no other girl had ever done so? Perhaps she'd just been playing hard to get — to stir him up a little? He'd get his own back if that were the case. There'd be all the time in the world later, after Tangier, and the child had been put on a 'plane. She'd go off somewhere with him — Morocco, maybe. He'd always fancied the atmosphere of a place like Morocco. And if Phil had any doubts, they'd go soon enough when she saw how much money he had. No girl could resist the temptation of mink and diamonds, cadillacs and yachts and any other god-damn thing in the world she fancied.

Phil could look pretty stunning when she was all dressed up. A little more sophistication and grooming and she'd be a worthy mistress to show off in the lush hotels and casinos of the world. She'd do anyway, until he found something he liked better.

He glanced at his watch.

'We're almost at Nice,' he said. 'We'll have to rush to get the 'plane.'

He was in no particular hurry himself but he could see the necessity of seeming anxious to reach Tangier at the earliest possible moment. The itinerary left him no time to dally with Phil on the way. He drew out the piece of paper and glanced at it irritably. The connection from Madrid for Tangier left at 7.10 p.m. — two hours would scarcely allow sufficient time for a seduction scene . . .

Jeff grinned to himself. It didn't matter. There'd be all the time in the world afterwards. They could put the child on the 'plane at Madrid in care of the air hostess and wire the Kingleys to meet it at Nice. By that time he and Phil would be on their way to . . .

'We're there!' Phil interrupted his thoughts. She glanced round the train carriage and felt a moment of panic wondering which of the other travellers was the detective promised by the inspector, to shadow them. Amongst the crowd of tourists, it was impossible to tell who had boarded the train with them at St. Raphael. Suppose the man had missed the train? She caught herself up sharply. That kind of thinking was absurd and she need have no fear — Charles said someone would be watching her all the time.

But on the 'plane to Madrid, she was again afraid. She had made a careful study of the faces in the cabin and not one bore any resemblance to the train passengers. Once more, her natural intelligence came to her support. There were probably a number of different detectives involved and the one accompanying them to Madrid could very well have taken over at the airport.

There were a number of dark-eyed Spaniards on the 'plane, looking like business men on their way back to Madrid. He could be any one of them.

She lay back with her eyes closed and tried to relax. Quite suddenly, she thought of home and Granny and her quiet uneventful life there. Now all this seemed reality and home just like a dream. Yet this fantastic journey to collect a kidnapped child from Tangier was more like the dream — or a nightmare. She had craved adventure and excitement but this was beyond anything she could have imagined. Life was very strange the way it had the power to catapult a person from one extreme to the other!

She shivered although it was not cold. She felt Jeff's eyes on her and longed once more for Greg — dear, safe Greg whom she could trust. If only it were *he* sitting beside her, flying with her to Madrid!

She must have slept a little despite her nerves, for when she next glanced round her, they were coming down to land. The excitement of seeing a new country — even if it were only the airport — was lost in her renewed nervousness now that they were so nearly at their destination. Supposing this was all some new and ghastly trick of Jeff's and Rupert was not waiting for them safe and unharmed? How could she ever face Suzanne and Charles if she were forced to return without him?

'For heaven's sake cheer up, Phil!' Jeff said crossly, as he shepherded her into the transit lounge and towards the bar. 'You look as if you were going to a funeral!'

She pulled herself together and forced a smile.

'I'm sorry — it's just that I can hardly believe we'll be seeing Rupert. Suppose . . . '

'Don't be such a little fool — of course he's all right. Stop thinking about him. Think about us — you and me. You know, Phil, I really don't feel inclined to rush madly back to Nice. I'd like to see something of Spain now we're actually in the place. What do you say to stopping on the way back for a few days — just you and me — do some sightseeing and have ourselves a good time?'

He spoke casually but there was an underlying edge to his voice and a narrowing of his eyes which warned Phil this was part of a preconceived plan.

'And Rupert?' she asked.

'We can put him on a 'plane for Nice. He'd be okay. Charles and Suzanne would meet him the other end.'

'Wouldn't they think it strange if you and I . . .'

'To hell with them!' Jeff broke in. 'Who cares what they think. That wretched island was a deadly bore, anyway. Believe me, Phil, you just don't know what life's about. I could show you around. You needn't worry about money — I've plenty enough for both of us. And if Suzanne fires you — so what? I'll take care of you.'

She pretended to consider it. In fact she was wondering what could be making Jeff so incautious. Perhaps the three brandies he'd downed one after another on the 'plane were making him careless. He could not seriously believe she was capable of falling in with such a plan?

'I suppose my dear little innocent is shocked!' He was taunting her now, teasing her in a way which always made her feel prudish and unworldly. Then she remembered that this mocking, handsome boy was responsible for Rupert's kidnapping and heaven knows what other evil and her fear gave way to something new — she despised him.

'How about it, honey?'

She was saved a reply by the man sitting next to Jeff. He addressed him first in Spanish and then in broken English, asking Jeff if he was a tourist and could maybe offer him some useful advice about Madrid.

Jeff bought the man a drink,

introduced Phil and became suddenly very garrulous. To Phil's horror, he was making it obvious to the stranger that Phil was his girlfriend and that they were off to Tangier on what Jeff chose to call 'a honeymoon'. The stranger winked and slapped Jeff on the back and the two men ordered more drinks. Jeff was rapidly getting drunk.

For a few moments, Phil wrestled with a new fear. Suppose Jeff became too drunk to carry through his plan to hand over the ransom money in Tangier and collect Rupert? But at this point, the stranger shot her a long deep glance and with an almost audible sigh of relief, she realised that this was no chance meeting after all. This was one of the plain clothes detectives promised by the inspector.

It was the new 'friend' who helped Jeff on board the 'plane for Tangier. As soon as they were airborne, he ordered black coffee for Jeff and succeeded in getting him partly sober, but not sober enough to be cautious.

'Let's have a party when we touch down!' the man said, still playing the part of a friendly acquaintance. 'We will have what you English call the night on the tiles, no?'

Jeff grinned stupidly.

'Not English — American. Girl's English!' he waved in Phil's direction. 'Frigid, cold as ice — that's her. Doeshunt love me.'

'Forget her!' the stranger said in a confidential whisper loud enough in fact for Phil to hear. 'You and me — we go together. I show you lovely warm-hearted girls in Tangier!'

Jeff grinned.

'Okay, okay. But firsht I gotta meet some friends. Verrry important — gotta meet my pals.'

Phil drew in her breath. How much more was Jeff going to reveal?

'Oh, no, we waste time. You meet friends later.'

'No, gotta meet friends firsht!' Jeff said doggedly. 'Airport Tangier. Won't take long — then we'll go and find a lot of lovely girls. You're a good friend — a swell friend. You unnersthand me. Not like her!' He pointed at Phil and made an ugly grimace. 'You'll be shorry — could have bought you anything . . . anything you wanted. Shorry — that's what you'll be!'

Quite suddenly, he fell asleep. Only then did Phil's hands unclench. The stranger did not move but wrote hurriedly on the back of an envelope and pushed it across to Phil.

There'll be five of our men at the airport. I expect the meeting will be in the arrivals lounge. He'll be sobered up when he wakes so watch your step. I won't be far off. The moment you have the child in your arms get out of the way. It could get rough when we move in.

She screwed up the paper and nodded her understanding. The palms of her hands were damp but now that there were only a few minutes to go before this would be all over and Rupert safe, she was no longer afraid — only excited.

'Will you fasten your safety-belts, please.'

At a glance from the detective, Phil leant over and shook Jeff by the arm.

'Jeff, we're there!' she said.

He opened his eyes and looked at her blankly. Then as she repeated her warning, he sat up and looked quickly down at his feet where he had put the briefcase containing all the money. He looked, too, at the detective who was feigning sleep; reassured that no one had touched his case while he slept off the brandy, he relaxed and grinned at Phil.

'Must have crashed out — all that booze on an empty stomach. Didn't say anything stupid, did I?'

Phil shook her head. He seemed to have forgotten what had passed between him and the stranger.

The 'plane landed and together with

the other passengers they went into the building. They lined up to go through customs and Jeff seemed suddenly nervous.

'Damn it!' he said. 'They may ask me to open this!' He indicated the brief-case. 'Never thought of that. Fool!' He seemed furiously angry with himself but the customs officer barely glanced at them and scribbled on the briefcase and their overnight cases without question.

Jeff was elated.

'Last hurdle cleared!' he whispered, taking her arm. 'Now for the pay-off,' he thought smugly, 'and Master Jeff Aymon has pulled off his first big coup!'

They reached the lounge and Phil stared round the room in a panic of anxiety. There was no sign of Rupert. Twice her eyes roamed past the dark, Spanish-looking couple with the small boy asleep in his mother's arms. Then her eyes went back to them — noticing something only subconsciously regis-tered at her earlier look — the child's head was a mass of golden, not black, curls.

'Jeff!' she gasped. 'Look — that's Rupert — I'm sure of it!'

Phil had to force herself to stay with Jeff — to approach the couple casually as if they were meeting friends. The man stood up pretending, none too skilfully, not to recognise Jeff. Then Jeff said in French:

'Monsieur Viellard? I was to meet someone of that name.'

The man nodded and looked down at the brief-case in Jeff's hand.

'You have the luggage?'

'Yes, indeed!' Jeff's face was amused. Unable to contain herself any longer, Phil said:

'May I see Rupert? If it really is Rupert . . .'

The woman held out the child who was in such a deep sleep that it could only have been drug induced. Phil grasped him and heard the deep slow breathing and tears of relief sprang to her eyes. It was Rupert — drugged, maybe, but alive. 'Suzanne!' she thought. 'If only I could hand him to you now.'

Suddenly she remembered the detective's note. She glanced at Jeff who seemed lost in conversation with the Frenchman. She began to edge slowly backwards, as if by accident, hoping the woman, who had so far not spoken a word, would not notice. But when she was no more than five feet away, the woman looked up and turned hurriedly to attract the Frenchman's attention. Phil abandoned caution and turned and ran as fast as she could with Rupert's weight in her arms, until she was amongst a milling crowd of people round the bar. When she looked back it was to see four men closing in a tight little circle round Jeff and his two companions. She saw Jeff at the moment he saw them; saw his face grow evil with anger and fear as he realised he had walked into a trap. Then, with a gasp of horror, she saw his hand go down to his pocket. At the same moment, the Frenchman put out a hand to prevent Jeff from reaching his gun; then the police closed round the group and she could see nothing more.

She closed her eyes, her heart thudding, her arms aching with Rupert's weight. A voice she knew said gently:

'It's all right, Miss Bethel — everything's all right. We've got both of them and the money.'

The detective from the 'plane was easing Rupert out of her trembling arms.

'I think we'll take the youngster to the First Aid room. He's probably drugged. You could do with a brandy, too!' He gave her a very English smile. 'Medicinal, of course!'

Much later, Phil was to puzzle over the fact that at this — one of the most satisfying and happy moments of her whole life — she had to burst into tears. Trying to explain it to Greg as they lay on the sands of Topaz Island two days later, she said:

'I suppose it was relief from tension.'

Greg turned over on his stomach and

picked up a handful of silver sand and let it sift slowly on to the golden brown of Phil's outstretched arm.

'I nearly cried when I saw you and Rupert get off that 'plane at Nice safe and sound!' he said. 'That was relief all right. You just don't know how worried I was, Phil. I nearly went out of my mind thinking of you gallivanting all over Europe with that — that creep!'

Phil laughed, then abruptly, stopped laughing.

'Jeff *was* a creep. What will happen to him, Greg? He'll go to prison, I suppose?'

Greg nodded.

'Unless Charles decides not to press charges but I think the police would have to anyway. I don't honestly know. And frankly, I don't much care.'

'At least no harm came to Rupert. *He* doesn't seem one tiny jot worse for his adventure.'

'The Spanish love children as a rule. It was lucky that Frenchman, Viellard, found a decent woman to look after him. That'll be something in his favour when the judge is handing out sentences.'

He brushed the little heap of sand off Phil's arm and bending his head, touched the soft golden brown skin with his lips. She smiled into his eyes and he said huskily:

'You know I love you, don't you, Phil?'

She nodded shyly.

Greg sighed.

'It'll be years before we get married, but when we do, we'll come somewhere like this on our honeymoon — somewhere hot and sunny and romantic, like Topaz Island.'

When she did not reply, he sat up and the dreamy, soft look left his face.

'Phil, you *are* going to marry me one day, aren't you?'

'Perhaps — I'm not sure!'

'But, Phil, last night . . . you said . . . *didn't you mean it?* . . . you said you loved me.'

She couldn't keep the serious expression on her face any longer. Jumping to her feet, she looked down at him, laughing.

'Of course I do . . . and of course I'll marry you . . . one day!' Then she turned and ran away from him, her tall slender figure a golden flash against the azure blue background of the sea.

For a moment, Greg watched her, caught in a single instant of immobility as if the beauty and radiance he saw in her held him tightly in some magic spell. Then the smile returned to his face and he jumped to his feet and began to run after her. Little by little, he gained on her until when they reached the dunes, they fell together, arms around one another, laughing and utterly contented, into the sand.

THE END